CUTTER
Director's Cut

j. woodburn barney

An AppalachianAcorn Book

ISBN-10: 1530468116
ISBN-13: 978-1530468119

Published by AppalachianAcorn

Cover design and illustration by Tad Barney

for Deborah
and for my kids, sired and acquired.

Maggie —
Thanks for thinking
of me! Hope you guys
enjoy
Jim

"And some that smile have in their hearts,

I fear, millions of mischiefs."

William Shakespeare, _Julius Caesar_

When my twin brother, J. Smith Barney, was reading my first book, *Cutter*, he wrote me and asked, "How much of this is true?" My response was, "I would like to think that it is all true, but if what you are asking is 'how much is factual?', then not very much." More than a few readers I know personally told me they sometimes got bogged down reading *Cutter* because they were trying to figure out who was who in real life. To each of them, I explained not one character was real. While they may have shared traits with some real person, or even uttered words a real person had said, they all were creations of a rabid imagination. Such is the case with this story. Do not look for anyone you know, including me or yourself.

CUTTER
Director's Cut

ONE

Jean Smith smiled. She finally had him. She had been absolutely positive the mayor was planning something which would betray the good folks of Columbus, Colorado. But until now she had no proof, only the suspicions of a bureaucrat who finds a snake under every political rock. And she had him recorded. Talking to someone about Riverside Park. Not that talking about a park was a crime or anything, but it was the mayor's tone. Jean could tell. He was up to no good.

Jean had managed to patiently work her way into a job in the mayor's office, putting in years of boring pencil-pushing labor, starting as a clerk in the Human Resources Office of Job Safety, eventually becoming an assistant safety officer and now was the safety officer for the mayor's office, a public trust she took very seriously. Though not as seriously as her civic responsibility to root out and expose those who would use their city positions to benefit themselves. Or their friends and relatives. Everyone else in the office just saw her as a pain in the ass. A pain in the ass who spent her time, and wasted city dollars, warning everyone about the dangers of paper cuts and reminding them not to lean back on two legs of a chair.

"Ruth, this is Jean," she whispered into her cell phone, though she was alone in her car.

"Hey," was the only response. Ruth was not happy to hear from Jean. Again. Ruth Roberts was the hatchet woman for the *Columbus City Times*, the best newspaper in the region. Naturally, since it was the only newspaper in the region. The editor, on direct orders from the publisher, kept Ruth on a tight chain to be released only when the publisher decided to wage war on someone in the community. As a result, Ruth was seen, at least by the unwashed masses, as a crusading reporter they could trust to find and lay bare the evil doers in the city. Most everybody in public service thought of her as just what she was, the publisher's personal Rottweiler. But everyone agreed they would rather have a task force of FBI and IRS agents knock on their doors than have Ruth start sniffing their trail.

Jean saw Ruth as her natural compatriot in the never-ending battle against the forces of evil. Ruth saw Jean as another one of those crazy paranoids she had to dismiss on a daily basis. Sadly, because Jean worked in the mayor's office and might accidently stumble over something of real use to her, Ruth couldn't tell Jean to fuck off. Which is what Ruth told the other crazies.

"Listen, Ruth, I have Mayor Humphrey on my recorder talking about Riverside Park and you have to hear it." Ruth groaned. Ah, shit, not the Jean Smith recorder. The first four or five times Jean had contacted Ruth about something newsworthy on her recorder, Ruth had listened. What Ruth learned was everybody in city government already knew about Jean's "secret" recorder. They all took turns making up stories they told loudly enough that even the cheap recorder could pick up. Stories that ranged from who was sleeping with whom to who was on the take to who participated in the post-council meeting orgy in the treasurer's office.

This was, however, the first time Jean claimed to have the mayor on tape. Ruth reluctantly agreed to meet her for coffee the next morning.

"Great. See you at Ross' at seven. Good night. And thanks." Jean was excited. Her big break. Finally everyone would know she was important. Besides her mom and dad. They already told her how important she was. And Suzie, Jean's significant other. Her life partner. At least until Suzie could find either a) a good job, or b) a new girlfriend with a good job. But Suzie always acted suitably impressed when Jean told her about her important work and the important people she knew and the important city inside information. Poor plain, drab, frumpy Jean. She did have a good heart. If she was just, just…Suzie didn't even know where she would start to give Jean a makeover. Inside or outside.

Jean closed the connection on her phone and slid it into her purse. This was going to be great. She couldn't stop smiling. Couldn't wait to get home and share the news with Suz. First she had to grab the materials for her eight o'clock presentation of her new "Safety in the Workplace" class at the Health Department. She'd have to go back to her office for those. Her office was in the City Hall Annex, unlike her coworkers who had offices right there in the granite and sandstone historical City Hall. Sorry, Miss Smith, we just don't have room here, but we have some really nice space in the Annex. Maybe now they would let her have an office in the real City Hall.

City Hall dated back to the 1890s, when Columbus was a small but thriving town on the Arkansas River. The town had been founded in 1880 by Christopher "Kit" Carroll when silver was discovered in the nearby mountains. Unlike many of the Colorado silver rush boomtowns, Columbus had actually flourished after the silver played out. Thanks in large part to Kit's understanding that sooner or later, every rush ended and only the folks who planned for that eventuality made any real money from the silver mania. So Kit put up cheap wooden gambling halls and bars and brothels and saved every penny, or more correctly, every bag of silver nuggets. With that he built substantial structures downstream, first a saw mill, then a bank, then a hotel, and then laid out a downtown and residential areas. By the 1890s, the silver was gone. He burned down the bars, the gambling dens and the whorehouses and turned the old town into a park, all six hundred acres of it. In time, the city grew around the park and its neighborhood became the center of community wealth.

Now Columbus was the third largest city in Colorado with a balanced economy which saw it through bad times and allowed it to thrive during the good ones. Kit had started things off well for the city, and his son Kit Junior did even better. The son bought up all the riparian rights for many miles up and down the Arkansas to control water access, convinced the state legislature to locate Central Western State University on land his family donated just west of downtown (of course, the family kept the land on all sides of the donation, since, who knows, maybe one day the state would need to buy some for expansion, which it did, at an inflated price) and gave the federal government land for the Office of Mining Oversight.

With that, Columbus had a guaranteed source of water and access to markets, it had a continuing source of bright young people, and it had a recession proof government business. Over the next seventy-five years new businesses started and flourished, so the city was now home to a major national insurance company, the biggest regional bank west of the Mississippi and a thriving data industry. When the mountain sports boom of the 60s began and flourished, Columbus' quaint downtown and proximity to world class skiing, hiking, biking, camping and golf insured that every year it was named a top ten place to live and work.

As patriarch of the family, Ty Carroll, great, great grandson of Kit, continued the family tradition of personally controlling all of the family businesses and interests. Which were plentiful. They owned controlling interest of the regional bank and the largest local health provider. They had a major share of the insurance company. They were the largest landholder and developer in the area. They owned the most popular local radio and television stations. And Ty himself served as publisher of the city's only newspaper. Most everyone agreed the Carroll family always had the best interests of the community at heart. Those who voiced concern about the power of the family soon found themselves being shunned by community leaders. At best. At worst, they found themselves the subject of a Ruth Roberts exposé.

When Ruth arrived at Ross' for her meeting with Jean, she knew she had to tread carefully. In the unlikely event Jean actually had some information which might be damaging to Mayor Humphrey. Every reporter at the paper was aware Humphrey had been endorsed by the paper. Which meant that he was handpicked by Ty Carroll. Not that it would make him off limits. She just needed to be astute. After all, Ty had not called her about Humphrey.

Ruth ordered coffee and toast. It arrived before Jean did. Ruth finished her meager breakfast and still no Jean. By seven thirty Ruth gave up, packed up her laptop and cell phone and paid the bill. Relieved that Jean had not showed. She thought it a little unusual though. Jean was the kind of person who so craved the spotlight and had so little to earn her a place in it, she would never miss an opportunity to have a reporter listen to her. Ruth suffered a brief moment of reporter angst, that sinking feeling in the pit of her stomach which came with the fear some other reporter might be getting her story instead. The moment passed. This was Jean Smith we were talking about. She had probably gotten up and listened to her recording again, realized she had nothing and was too embarrassed to show up.

6

Suzie had fallen asleep on the couch waiting for Jean to get home. Actually, drinking half a box of wine had caused her to pass out on the couch. She woke up a little after eight o'clock the next morning when Jean's office called to find out why she had not shown up for her presentation. Suzie told them to hold on and stumbled into the bedroom to get Jean. Not there.

"Sorry. Jean's gone already. She's probably on her way." With that, Suzie crawled into bed and fell back asleep. At noon, she was reawakened by the phone.

"Sorry to bother you again, Suzie, but this is Molly from Jean's office. We still haven't heard from her and I was getting a little worried. She isn't answering her cell phone or responding to text messages. Do you know where she might be?"

Lots of fuzz in her eyeballs. And in her brain. Cotton in her mouth. "Uh. Just a second. Let me check. Uh. Hold on," Suzie managed. She sat up, rubbed her temples and slowly got out of bed. Checked the rest of the cabin and looked outside. No Jean. No Jean car. Became aware that there might be a problem. Damn. "She's not here. Her car is gone and there is no note," Suzie said into the phone. "I'll try calling her. Let me know if she contacts you guys, Molly." She hung up without saying goodbye.

After she tried to call Jean, with no response, Suzie brushed her teeth, threw some water on her face and dressed in jeans and her heavy sweater. Started a pot of coffee. It was early October so the temperature could be anywhere between eighty and zero. It was closer to zero

7

with some snow on the ground around the cabin. Their cabin, located off Route 82 about twenty-five miles from downtown Columbus, was almost in the shadow of Mt. Elbert, the highest peak in Colorado at 14,433 feet. At over 9,000 feet the cabin spent much of its time in winter. Suzie started her beat up Trailblazer to let it warm up and went back inside.

While she drank a cup of coffee, she called Jean's folks. They hadn't heard from her. As soon as she asked about Jean, she knew she had made a mistake. Jean's mother, a worrier by inclination and training, started wailing and moaning. Suzie tried to calm her down and told her she would find Jean and call them as soon as she did and told Momma Smith not to worry. Right. She then checked in with a couple of their in-town friends. No one had heard a thing.

She drove into town, checked at the hospital and at the places Jean might go, like the bookstores near the University. No one had heard or seen a thing. Finally she called the sheriff's office and was told they couldn't do anything until twenty-four hours had elapsed, but they said they would send a patrol car out to check the route between City Hall and the cabin. About three miles shy of the cabin, they found skid marks that led them to Jean's car at the bottom of a gulch. Jean had gone over the embankment, the car had flipped numerous times, and Jean had died of a broken neck, still strapped into her seat belt and with the airbag deployed. A proper safety officer to the very end.

Although Jean didn't appear to have many friends while she was alive, her funeral filled the church. The mayor had ordered his staff to attend, there were a few other coworkers and the LBGT community was well represented, having lost one of their own. Momma Smith, who had prepared to loudly lament the passing of her daughter, was so surprised by the turnout, she could only weep quietly. Her daughter, it turned out, must have been important to have so many people show up for her funeral. And Mayor Humphrey himself delivered the eulogy. While she was beside herself with sadness, she was also very proud and for years afterwards told people how important her Jean had been.

Suzie, of course, felt very bad. Not so much because Jean had died, but because she wasn't sure how she was going to pay next month's rent. She had just assumed that her meal ticket would be there as long as she needed her. With winter coming on, this could be very difficult. She hadn't saved any money and by this time of the season, the ski resorts would have already done their hiring. Jean's city life insurance had covered the funeral expenses and left two thousand dollars more but that wouldn't go very far. Since Jean's car had actually been owned by her parents, the car insurance money went to them.

So Suzie was ecstatic to learn Jean had bought a life insurance policy which named Suzie as the sole beneficiary. And Jean hadn't skimped. The policy was for one hundred thousand dollars, with double indemnity if the death was accidental. Which it was. Or so the insurance company decided after they did a thorough investigation and determined that, while they would like to claim it was a suicide and not have to pay anything, the skid marks proved otherwise. Suzie was not going to have to work for a long, long time. With the added advantage of never having to listen to Jean Smith again.

A couple of months later, Suzie was snowed in at the cabin, beginning to suffer from the cold and the loneliness. Ready to shoot her television. Actually missing Jean. When her phone rang, she couldn't figure out what the sound was. Been too long since she heard from anyone. Finally it sunk in and she pounced on the phone. "Hello?"

"Hello. Is this Suzie Morgan?"

"Yes it is. Who's this?"

"My name is Ruth Roberts. I'm a reporter with the *Columbus City Times.*"

"Oh, yeah. I know your name. You were a friend of Jean's. Right?" Suzie asked.

Ruth was surprised by the question. Friend? I don't think so, lady. I thought your girlfriend was bat shit crazy. That was what Ruth thought. What she said was, "Yes. Yes, I was. Terrible loss. My heart goes out to you."

"Thanks. It has been rough. What can I do for you?" Suzie wondered, secretly hoping that maybe Ruth was calling to ask her out.

"I was wondering, when you went through Jean's personal effects, did she happen to leave a small recorder?

The day she died, I was supposed to meet her to listen to something she had recorded," Ruth explained. What she left unsaid was that while her brain told her there was nothing of any use, her reporter paranoia had been screaming at her for two months, "WHAT WAS ON THAT RECORDING???"

"No," Suzie answered. "I went through all her stuff with her parents and I wondered about that myself. She was never without that recorder. We just assumed it was lost in the wreck or thrown out after they gave her office to her replacement. Sorry. I could call you if it turns up."

"Thanks. That would be great. Sorry to bother you," and Ruth gave Suzie her number and signed off.

Shit. Stupid bitch. Jean was still a pain in her ass.

TWO

"Christ in a handbasket!"

"Winston Weller Williams, how many times do I have to remind you not to use that kind of language around the kid?!?"

"Sorry, Babe. I just pinched the shit, uh, er, crap out of my finger. Sorry," Cutter yelled down to his wife. Cutter, who hated his given name of Winston, especially the way his wife Sandy used it, was having a major battle trying to assemble a Swedish-designed crib using directions written by an American sadist. Whatever happened to simple nuts and bolts or wood screws? There was something intrinsically wrong with a culture which made things more difficult. Like beer. A guy had to play twenty questions just to order a goddamn beer these days.

Sandy yelled up the stairs, "Hey, don't forget we have a meeting at ten. I'll take Jordan to school but be at the office by nine-thirty, okay?" Jordan, who had just turned six and was in kindergarten, was Sandy's daughter and had been adopted by Cutter when they married two years earlier. Jordan was very excited about getting a new little brother, although, as she told her mom, a little sister would have been much better. By the time Sandy collected her things, Jordan was standing at the door, coat on and backpack over her shoulder.

Jordan yelled up the stairs, "Bye, Daddy. Love you. Work hard today."

From upstairs, "Bye-bye, Shortcakes. Love you too." Cutter did. In fact he was as crazy about the kid as he was about the mother. He had known Sandy for eight years, the first two as coworkers at the City of Davenport, Iowa, through the time of her affair that resulted in Jordan, and then later when they started a consulting business together. Though partners on the letterhead, in actuality, Sandy provided the brains and business savvy. Left Cutter to handle the chutzpah. It worked well for them. What started out as mutual admiration for each other's skills somehow managed to turn to attraction, then to lust, then to love. Cutter was still pretty amazed by it all.

Thirty minutes later, Cutter had had enough of the crib, said, "Fuck it," and decided the baby could just sleep in a drawer. It had been good enough for him; it'd be good enough for his kid. Of course, Cutter was one of the younger kids from a family with eight children, so that had been the only place they had for him. Still, he wouldn't have traded his childhood for anything. He wanted to give Jordan and their son the same experience growing up. But with their own beds. Decided he would tackle the crib again tonight. Maybe Sandy could show him how.

He got ready for work. Sandy had convinced him that he needed to keep his wild, curly, blond hair neatly trimmed, but she would never get him out of his jeans and sweater. He had sworn after his stint in Davenport City Hall he would never wear a suit again. So far, he had kept his vow. He showered, shaved, dressed in his

13

meeting-potential-clients jeans and corduroy jacket and drove to their office in suburban Des Moines. He even managed to arrive before nine-thirty. Sandy was already at her desk working.

At a few minutes before ten, their shared receptionist, Kathy Jones, called Sandy's phone. "Mr. Stalter is here to see you."

"Thanks. Cutter will be out in a minute to get him. Would you please offer him a cup of coffee or something else to drink?"

"You bet," Kathy chirped and hung up.

Two minutes later Cutter walked into the lobby wearing his aw-shucks grin and stuck out his hand, "Mr. Stalter, I'm Cutter Williams. Welcome to our firm. Let's go back to see Sandy."

Hugh Stalter was a short but trim, balding man in his mid-sixties, nicely dressed and very well groomed. A professional. He got to his feet, shook Cutter's hand and collected his briefcase. "Very pleased to meet you. Strange name, Cutter. How'd you get it?"

"Long story. I'll tell you sometime," Cutter replied as he led the way down the hall to Sandy's office.

Sandy stood as they walked into her office. When Stalter noticed her pregnant belly, his smile disappeared. "Oh, you're pregnant," he stammered. "I didn't know."

Sandy flashed a big grin. "Yes I am," she said. "Luckily it doesn't diminish my ability to think and work."

Now Stalter was completely flustered. "No. No. That's not what I meant." He was blushing, completely embarrassed by his reaction. "I'm sorry. I was just surprised. I

14

came here hoping to offer you a job and your being pregnant might present a problem for you. Sorry. I don't mean a problem for you, but, you know, a problem for…"

Cutter tried to salvage the conversation, "Sandy is pretty clever. She can actually chew gum, work and be pregnant all at the same time. What's the job?" He and Sandy were by now totally amused by this guy. "And please, have a seat."

Stalter sat. Or more precisely, collapsed into the chair offered. Cutter and Sandy sat side by side on the couch. Cutter put his hand on his wife's belly and patted it. She pushed it away. But smiled. Sandy tried again, "So what can we do for you, Mr. Stalter?"

Stalter gathered himself. "Again, I'm sorry for my reaction. I was, uh, nonplussed. No excuse. I am the chairman of the Parks and Recreation Commission in Columbus, Colorado. We have a rather unique situation in Columbus. Years ago, one of our previous mayors used the parks department to hire all of his political cronies and his extended family. The parks were a mess, dirty, trashy and unsafe. It all came to a head when one of the mayor's nephews got drunk and drove a tractor mower into a family of picnickers, and one of the children died in the accident. The good citizens of Columbus had had enough.

"They drafted a petition to amend the city charter, got enough signatures for it to go on the ballot, and it passed by a huge majority. What that amendment did was create a nonpolitical commission of unpaid citizens to oversee the administration of the parks. Not to brag, but we have built quite a parks and recreation department since then. We have won three National Gold Medal awards, the highest award in our industry, and have had several directors who are local legends. Our department is always mentioned among the chief reasons Columbus is a top ten place to live."

"Pretty impressive," Sandy offered. "How can we possibly help you?"

"Well, to be blunt, I'm not sure you can. Now," Stalter answered.

Cutter was on his feet quickly, extending a hand toward Stalter, "Well, thanks for coming in. Let us know if there is a time we can help you." Uncharacteristically, Cutter was not being sarcastic.

"No, no," Stalter waved him down. "Again, I'm sorry. I'm not usually this obtuse." Cutter sat and rolled his eyes. "Let me explain. A lot better, hopefully. And hopefully you can give me some direction. My cohorts and I are desperate."

"We'll try," Sandy told him, and she gave Cutter her sit-boy-and-stay look.

"About six months ago, our director, Bob Wayne, came to us to tell us the mayor of Columbus, a gentleman named Carleton Humphrey, was putting pressure on him to share control of the parks with the mayor's office. Bob had been a long-time department employee who rose through the ranks. Frankly, he wasn't the brightest director we'd ever had, but he had put in his time. He couldn't put his finger on what the mayor wanted, though. He just felt pressure. Since he couldn't tell us what he wanted done, we couldn't help. The problem seemed to go away."

"But?" Cutter asked.

"Not so much a 'but', more of an 'oh, shit'. Pardon my French." He blushed again.

"I live with Cutter. Think nothing of it," Sandy smiled.

"Anyway," Stalter continued, "three weeks ago, I got a call from the police chief. A heads up to let me know that they were going to arrest Bob that evening. I asked 'for what' and was told 'theft of public funds and malfeasance'. Seems that, at the mayor's request, the police had been following Bob for the previous month. Turns out our Director Wayne had a young girlfriend whom he put on the payroll. Only thing was, the time she was supposed to be working, they were actually shacked up in a motel. Over the last two years, she had been paid over forty thousand dollars and had done exactly zero hours of work."

"What happened?" Sandy asked.

"Bob asked us if he could just pay the money back and go on, as in no harm, no foul. We fired him."

This story was turning interesting. Cutter went on, "And?"

"Then things got downright weird. I got a call the mayor wanted to meet with the entire commission. That day. I called them together and we met. Even though our meetings are covered by state open meetings laws, when the mayor got there, he asked the recording secretary to leave and had his bodyguard lock the door from the outside, where he stood guard. Mayor Humphrey then said to us, and I quote as clearly as I remember, 'Your boy Bob is finished. He is going to jail. I am going to assume control of the department and will appoint a new director. From now on, you all work for me'."

"What did you say?" Sandy wondered.

"I said, and this quote is quite accurate, 'Fuck you.' Again, excuse my French. The mayor then told us that we either would go along with him, or the newspaper would start a campaign to get rid of a separate commission. Told us we had forty-eight hours to accept his proposal."

"I take it you didn't," Cutter suggested.

"Nope, we didn't. We met and to a person decided that it was our department, and we would continue to run it. Even if it meant taking on the newspaper."

Sandy wanted to know, "How many of you are there? Can you all afford a battle with a newspaper? There's a saying that you should never get into a fight with someone who buys ink by the barrel."

"So I've heard. There are nine of us, three appointed by a majority of the City Council, three by the probate court and three by the Council of Social Services. Each appointment is for six years and the appointments are staggered. It would be almost impossible for any one person or body to gain control of the commission. No one has ever tried. Until now. None of us is in a position that the paper could hurt badly, not if we stick together. Which I believe we will."

"What about you?" Cutter again.

"Nope. I'm retired," Stalter, a funny little smile on his face. Sandy and Cutter later learned that Hugh Stalter had been the Athletic Director at Central Western State University but had stepped down a couple of years earlier, at the request of the president of the university. Not that Hugh had done anything wrong. In fact, he had to resign because he had done exactly the right thing. CWSU had a very popular basketball coach, Rob "Fastbreak" Fellure who had taken the university to the Final Four twice, after his legendary career there as a player. Fastbreak was a local hero. Unfortunately, Fastbreak decided to punch out one of his own players during a game on national television. Conduct unbecoming. Hugh called him in and fired him. After six months of being hounded by major donors, the university president quietly asked for Hugh's resignation. Hugh was no dummy. He retired. With honors. And a very nice pension.

"So what do you need from us?" Sandy asked.

Stalter looked directly at Sandy and said, "I came here to ask you to be our next director."

Sandy looked confused and said, "I don't understand. You know we are a consulting firm, right?"

"I do. One of the commissioners is Dr. Kaitlyn Reinan, a professor of education at the university. Katie apparently did a research study on the Davenport Community Scholarship Program and came away very impressed with you. We checked around and could find only the highest recommendations for you and for your work. Frankly, Sandy, we have to hire someone from the outside, someone with no community agenda, someone who we hope won't be swayed by local politics. We know from experience that hiring a parks person from some other jurisdiction won't work. Those 'professionals' aren't really; the directors who move around seem to be only interested in resume building, not community building."

"But I have no parks experience. And the closest Cutter ever got was working at a golf club and working on a fishing boat."

"Hey, don't forget when I was in high school, I spent a lot of time parking, too," Cutter chimed in. They both ignored him.

"Which makes you perfect in our eyes," Stalter went on. "But we need someone immediately. Someone, I'm afraid, who is able to devote as many hours each week as needed to make a go of it. I'd guess that will be sixty hours or so a week for the first six to twelve months. I think we would feel very uncomfortable asking a woman who is having a baby to make that commitment."

Cutter was thinking about the money. "If Sandy could work this out, how much would this contract pay? Our firm is not inexpensive, you know."

"Oh, we can't hire her on a contract. Sandy would have to be hired as a regular city employee at a director's rate of pay," and Stalter mentioned a figure.

"Geez," Cutter responded, "I'm sorry, but that isn't even in the ballpark."

Stalter held up his hand. "Believe me, we know. We vetted your firm enough to know how much you charge and that your clients think you're worth every penny. In fact several told us they thought you were a great deal. That's why another of our commissioners came up with a plan to also hire you on a consulting basis. The commissioner is also chair of the community arts organization, and his company would make a donation which would allow the arts folks to offer you a substantial contract. With a housing allowance, of course." He mentioned an additional figure.

Cutter blew out a low whistle.

"Though it is a moot point, right?" continued Stalter.

This time it was Sandy who held up her hand. "Maybe we can work something out." She raised her eyebrows toward Cutter who gave her the slightest nod.

Stalter moved forward in his chair. Scratched his bald head and asked, "What do you mean?"

"The truth of the matter is, you really wouldn't want me in that kind of role. I'm not always good at working with people. My expectations of what people should do sometimes exceed their willingness and their abilities."

"What Sandy is trying to say is that she can be a real bitch," Cutter added, then smiled. "But she's my bitch." She elbowed him hard enough that he grunted.

"I prefer perfectionist," Sandy explained. "When we go into organizations to help, I do the program planning part. Cutter handles the people part: training, cajoling, explaining, encouraging, getting buy-in, leading if need be. I really don't get it, how he seems to get folks to want to help him. Believe me, if I could figure out how to do that, I could fire him." She patted him on the knee.

"I'm not sure I'm following," Stalter said.

"Well, Cutter and I would need to discuss the idea at length, but what would you say to reversing our roles? Hire Cutter and I get the consulting contract, and you would still get me, though indirectly. And Junior here," she patted her stomach, "wouldn't be a problem."

"I don't know, Ms. Williams. I would have to talk to the other commissioners first. We would have to vet Mr. Williams as well. I do have to admit it is an enticing proposal, especially for a desperate man."

Sandy rose. "Why don't we meet tomorrow afternoon and decide if it's a fit?" she asked. She offered her hand to Stalter, who stood and shook it.

"Fine idea. Shall we say three o'clock?"

"Perfect," Sandy responded and she turned to Cutter. "I'll walk Hugh out and be back in a couple of minutes." Cutter knew this was pregnantspeak for "I gotta pee".

He shook Stalter's hand and said, "See you tomorrow. Thanks for coming in."

Ten minutes later, Sandy walked back in her office to find Cutter stretched out on the couch. He grinned at her. "Cutter Williams, Director of Parks and Recreation. Has a nice ring to it, doesn't it." He made it a statement, not a question. "Of course, I'd expect you to share your consulting fee, seeing as how it is so much more." Sandy snorted. They had decided within a few months of getting married that Sandy needed to control all of the family finances, right after she discovered he had not paid his auto insurance for over a year and had been driving uninsured and risking everything they owned. He

22

had had no defense. So he was allowed to have a debit card and a credit card, both with low limits. Even Jordan knew not to ask dad to buy something because he never had any money.

"Be serious, Cutter. I'm not sure how I feel about moving to the middle of the Rockies, but this might actually work for us. It would sure give me a lot more flexibility with the kids, and we wouldn't have to worry about the up and down of consulting income."

In fact, Cutter was already way into the idea. He hadn't really put words to it, but he was getting bored with the consulting thing and had thought that running something, being the boss, might be a fun thing to do. Like he wanted to leave his a mark on something. A dog pissing on a hydrant. Not so much about being important, but actually doing a real job, not just the hand holding he did now. Not to mention it had taken him two minutes on the internet to discover Columbus Parks owned three golf courses, and he had heard how far you could hit a golf ball in the thin mountain air. Sandy would have a hard time talking him out of it.

They spent the evening searching the internet for information about Columbus, its city government and the people who ran the town. Actually, Sandy did the research. Cutter had already decided and wanted to find nothing to dissuade him. He played with Jordan until he put her to bed and then continued his battle with the crib. He finally realized he would just have to take the damn thing apart if they were going to move. So he quit and counted it as a victory over the Swedes.

23

About midnight he went downstairs and found Sandy sitting on the couch, staring into space. He knew better than to interrupt. This was the most crucial part of Sandy making a decision. He marveled at it, her ability to sort through innumerable bits of data, pick out what was important, assemble it in a way most folks could never do, and come up with a solution. As a would-be writer, he understood creativity enough to be both in awe of her talent and jealous of it. Jealous in an admiring way.

He got himself a glass of wine, read the paper and waited. Half an hour later Sandy came out of her trance, looked at him and smiled. "It will work. Our families probably won't be wild about it, especially with Junior on the way, but we're a couple of hours away by car now and will be a couple of hours by plane then. Only question I have is whether you really want to take on a fifty hour plus, go in every day, under the gun position. You think you really want that?"

"Yep. Time for me to wear some big boy pants." He got up, patted her tummy and cocked his head toward the stairs. "Wanna go up and be serviced?"

"Uh huh. I do."

THREE

When Cutter came downstairs the next morning, he found Sandy and Jordan giggling at the kitchen counter.

"What's so funny?" he wondered as he searched for his favorite coffee mug, the one from the Oasis Restaurant in Fort Myers. Mostly he cared not about souvenirs, or for that matter, any of his possessions, but when Sandy had accidentally broken the handle off his mug, he was apoplectic. Sandy honestly thought he might cry. Until she showed him it was okay by mending it with super glue. She dreaded the day something happened to his precious golf clubs, God forbid. He found the stained cup, rinsed out yesterday's coffee sludge and poured a fresh cup. Tousled Jordan's hair, patted Sandy's stomach, said good morning to Junior and sat down with them.

"Daddy, we're moving to the mountains. I'm going to learn to ski and ride horses and everything." Then Jordan's huge grin disappeared and she turned to her mother. "We get to take Daddy with us, don't we?" She was totally serious.

"Of course we do, honey. We couldn't leave him here by himself. You know he'd get in trouble if we did that," Sandy reassured her and the grin returned.

"So moving to the mountains will be alright with you?" Cutter asked.

"Well, I'll miss some of my friends, mostly Sarah, but Mommy says she can come visit and that I'll make new ones there. And I get to go skiing!"

"Great! At least that's settled. Go get your suitcase, Shortcakes, and I'll meet you at the car. The sooner we start, the sooner we'll be there," Cutter told her. Jordan looked at her mom who smiled and shook her head.

"Daddy's just kidding you."

"Daddy, you are so silly. We have to pack all our stuff before we can move."

"Oh, yeah. I forgot. So you might as well go to school this morning."

Sandy started her round of morning orders. "Honey, go get your jacket and backpack so we can leave in a few minutes. Cutter, you need to haul butt. We have to have a proposal drawn up before our meeting with Hugh and you have to write it."

Jordan looked at Cutter and put her hand over her mouth, "Oh, Mommy said 'butt'. That means you better hurry."

"You betcha, Shortcakes. See you tonight. I love you. Have fun at school." With that, Cutter was on his feet, poured a second cup of coffee and disappeared back up the steps. "See you at the office, Babe."

At one thirty, Cutter walked into Sandy's office. "I just emailed you the proposal. Let me know what changes you want and I'll get copies made."

She pulled up the document, read it once quickly and then went through it a little more slowly. She gave him about a dozen "change-this, add-this, delete-this's" and told him, "Not bad. I think we've covered our asses well enough, with all the 'outs' we might need."

In a perfect imitation of Jordan, Cutter put his hand over his mouth and said, "Oh, Mommy said 'asses'. Someone's in trouble now." Sandy threw a paper clip at him and told him to get to work.

At a few minutes after three, Cutter led Hugh Stalter back into his wife's office. Without being asked, Hugh, who looked a little more frayed than the day before, sat on the couch, spread his knees apart and rested his elbows on his knees. He bowed his head and stared at the carpet, a shine coming off his bald head. He sighed.

"Rough night?" Cutter asked.

Hugh looked up and smiled. "No. Not at all. Kind of a long night though. Especially for a retired man." Now he grinned. "Spent a lot of hours on the phone, chasing down information on you. It was like following a treasure map. Every person we talked to about you seemed to know a different version. There's a campaign manager who thinks you are 'Aces' and a CFO who believes you are a buffoon. A bishop who thinks you walk on water—quite a statement for a Catholic bishop to make—and a former mayor who said you weren't loyal; a fishing boat captain who loves you and a high school principal who swears you are the devil incarnate. And that principal works for that bishop. Go figure."

"Good to know that fucking Fenton still remembers," thought Cutter.

"So what have you decided?" Sandy wanted to know.

"I talked at length with the other commissioners, and we all agreed the map led us back to where we started. It's you we want, Sandy, and if he," Stalter nodded his head at Cutter, "is what we have to take to get you, so be it. We will either win big, or if it all goes to hell in a handbasket, excuse my French, well, then we figure we can just push him," indicating Cutter again, 'under the bus'."

Sandy laughed. "I can't tell you how many times I've had that very same thought, Hugh. So far it has served me well."

"Hey guys, I'm right here, you know," Cutter interjected. He sounded a little miffed, but neither Sandy nor Hugh seemed to care. They had already decided it was a deal.

Three days later, dressed in his new blazer and nice jeans, Cutter was on a plane bound for Chaffee County International Airport, qualified as international only on the basis of four flights a week in winter direct to Mexican coast towns for the jet set to alternate skiing with beaching. Hugh sat next to him. It was April, what the Columbus tourism folks referred to as "a shoulder season" between skiing and golfing, their euphemism for the periods of the year when tourism died a violent death. As a result, there were very few passengers on this Saturday morning flight. Cutter stared out the window as they approached the Rockies and was a little rattled by the starkness of the mountains. White caps surrounded by immense spaces of nothing but brown and gray. Wondered if he could live without green.

Hugh interrupted his reverie. "You understand the agenda for the next two days? Any questions?" Hugh sounded as if he were not convinced he had done the right thing, selling the rest of the commission on this unknown commodity.

"I think so," Cutter answered. "Tonight we meet with the commission members. I assume we should give them one last chance to bail, eh?"

Cutter could see Hugh relax. Hugh's bald head bobbed up and down. "Yeah. I mean, a deal's a deal, but it would be wise to give them veto power. If they say 'no', we'll still pay all your costs and a consulting fee. Say, forty hours. That fair?"

"Fair enough. But they'll love me," Cutter reassured him. "After all, I am married to Sandy." Back to the schedule, "If I pass muster, you introduce me on the local *Meet the Press* type television show Sunday morning and announce the appointment. Before the mayor or the newspaper can react, I'll be on the job."

"That's the idea. I hate to appear so devious, and it will probably put you in an awkward position with the mayor, but we think this is best." Hugh finally smiled.

The pilot announced the beginning of the descent into Chaffee County and Cutter returned his attention to the mountains outside the window. He was happy to see green trees in the mountains and the green valley of the Arkansas as they made their final approach for landing.

He even managed a smile when he saw two golf courses with their characteristic bright green fairways standing out from the brown scrub land.

They made the seventeen mile drive north to downtown Columbus in silence. Cutter checked into his hotel and agreed to meet Hugh in the lobby at seven so they could arrive at the meet-and-greet together. Hugh shook his hand one more time and told him how grateful he was that this had worked out. Hugh left and Cutter went for an explore of the downtown. An explore which lasted a whole two blocks before he found a microbrewery. Decided learning the local beer was an excellent place to start learning the community.

"Good afternoon, sir. Welcome to Aspen Ridge Brewery." The waitress was cowgirl perky, from her multicolored boots to her fringed vest to her straw cowboy hat. "Would you like to see our list of beers and ales?" And she handed him a two page beer menu before he could say "just a beer." She turned on her heel and left the table. Two minutes later she was back. "Do you have any questions?"

"Why, yes, I do. Thank you. Could you tell me about your different beers?" Cutter had already decided that the Aspen Ridge lager was the closest thing to just a regular beer he would find. Although she started by describing the lager, he let her go through the entire list before saying, "I'll have that first one you mentioned." She nodded and smiled and walked away. He swore he could hear her whisper, "Asshole." Made him smile. I'm gonna love this place. He drank one beer (have to meet the new bosses) and after reconsidering starting off here as a jerk, he left a ten dollar tip. What he didn't hear after he left was, "Asshole rich guy."

At seven o'clock, the recording secretary sent out a notice to the public, in accordance with open meeting laws, that a meeting to discuss personnel matters would be held that night at the Founders Hotel downtown at eight. At the very same time, Hugh met Cutter in the lobby and they walked up to the Frontier Room where the rest of the commission was assembling. The two got a drink at the bar (sponsored by the Chairman of the Arts Council, Geren Randolph, who also happened to be the president of the second largest bank in the city) and Hugh then walked Cutter around and introduced him individually to each commissioner. Sandy had been right. Memorizing all their names beforehand was a good idea. He borrowed a trick he had learned from his old boss, the mayor of Davenport. Cutter would touch an arm or shoulder here, lean in for a conversation there, use both hands for a handshake with someone else. Something to make everyone feel special.

It worked. By ten minutes until eight, Cutter, using his very best aw-shucks smile, asked for everyone's attention, thanked them for inviting him to visit them and told them that if any one of them had any reservations, the deal was off. "Any questions? Comments?" All he got in response was nodding heads and smiles. Finally, Hugh said, "I do have a question, but it can wait until after the meeting."

31

At exactly eight o'clock, Hugh called the meeting to order. By 8:02, Winston Weller Williams was the new Columbus Parks and Recreation Director, by unanimous vote. By 8:03, the meeting was adjourned. By 8:04, everyone was headed back to the bar. At 8:08, Hugh asked Cutter, "So, how'd you get that nickname?"

"Actually, it's sort of parks and recreation related. I was a pretty decent baseball player when I was young. Started in little league, like most kids, played lots of positions, turned out I could throw pretty hard. By the end of Babe Ruth league, I was a full-time pitcher. Good enough that in high school I was starting varsity by ninth grade, though I only had three pitches, the fast ball, the change-up and a sweeping curve. The high school coach taught me how to throw a screwball and a cut fastball. The cutter was my go-to pitch, enough to earn me all-state honors. Got looked at by a few big league scouts. One of them, in an interview with the local press couldn't remember my name, so he called me 'Cutter'. It stuck."

By this point in the story most of the commissioners were listening. Geren, Jerry to his friends, asked Cutter, "Did you go any further? With baseball, I mean."

Cutter looked down and slowly shook his head. "Nope. Never had the chance. That screwball Coach taught me. Turns out it's called that because it screws up your arm. After half a season of college ball, my arm sprung a leak and never healed. Career over."

"Ah, that's too bad," Dr. Reinan interjected, sounding genuinely sorry for him. Made Cutter feel a little guilty

32

for telling them a story. But when she added, "At least we've hired someone who understands sports," he grinned.

Cutter made the rounds of thanking each commissioner individually and handed each his business card with his personal cell phone number. Told each to call any time they had a question or needed something. Another of Sandy's ideas. Took his leave, went back to his room, broke out the honor bar (hey, it was on the business account) and called Sandy.

"Hello, Mrs. Parks and Recreation Director."

"I take it things went well?" she asked.

"Just like you thought. Jordan still up?"

"No, she fell asleep a few minutes ago. Any surprises?"

"None," he replied. "Wham bam, thank you ma'am. I even gave them a chance to back out. Nine votes, nine yes's. Only question I got was how I got my name."

"Oh, Cutter, don't tell me. You didn't." She knew she should've explicitly told him "no stories!"

"They enjoyed it," was his only defense. They chatted for a few minutes, and he gave her the web address where she could watch his press conference live the next morning, exchanged "I love you's" and said good night.

Cutter arrived at the station early, dressed in khakis and his brand new green Columbus Parks and Recreation golf shirt, the one with the logo that looked like a soccer ball perched atop a snow covered mountain. As much as he hated coats and ties, he hated the logo even more. Not that Cutter was a fashion plate, but the only logos he would wear were on shirts from golf courses he

33

liked. And even then, they had to be small. Unlike this monstrosity.

Once again, he was greeted by Hugh. And a strange little man, wiry and dark skinned, with features that defied racial classification. And age. Might be thirty-five, might be sixty-five. Cutter couldn't tell if he was African-American, Native American, Hispanic or what. Hell, he might even be Native Australian. The guy wore a big smile and had so much energy, just standing, that Cutter thought he might start skipping around the station lobby.

"Cutter, I would like you to meet Hammond Eggleston, President of Columbus City Council. Better known as Ham and Eggs. Longtime friend of parks and longtime political foe of Carleton Humphrey."

Hammond grabbed Cutter's hand and started shaking it furiously. "Pleased to meet you, Son. Hugh has told me all about you. And your wife. Can't wait to meet her. So glad to have you here. Understand you are a baseball player. Or were. Other sports? Golf maybe?" He talked so fast Cutter could barely follow him. He sure didn't know which statement or question to respond to.

"A pleasure to meet you, President Eggleston," Cutter began.

"Ham and Eggs, Son. Ham and Eggs. Call me Ham and Eggs. Everyone does," Hammond interrupted. "We'll have plenty of time to chat later. Let's get this interview thing done first. The guy interviewing you, us, is the husband of Cherie Stone, on your board. You met her last night. President of the Columbus Area Garden

34

Society. Stoney will only throw you some lobs. Any question you don't want to, or can't, answer, just nod to us and Hugh or I will take it. Got it?"

By this point, Cutter could only bob his head up and down.

There weren't any questions aimed at Cutter he couldn't handle. Ham and Eggs had been right. This was a fluff piece for the reporter. Obviously a friend of Parks. Cutter alternated between his aw-shucks and serious *persona*e and told them how much he was looking forward to the job, to the city, to the nice folks of the community and blah, blah, blah. Half an hour later they were in the lobby, Ham and Eggs asking if they wanted to go to lunch. Before Cutter could answer, his cell phone vibrated in his pocket. He excused himself.

"You did good, sailor," Sandy said. "What's with the council president? Good guy?"

"Yeah, I think he is. Interesting, anyway. I'm off to lunch with him now."

"Jordan wants to say hi first."

Cutter waited while Sandy gave her daughter the phone. "Hi, Daddy. Have you been skiing yet? Did you ride a horse? Do you miss me?"

"No. No. And yes, terribly. I have to go, Shortcakes, but I'll call tonight. I promise." They said their goodbyes and hung up.

Cutter turned to the still grinning councilman and said, "Lunch? I'm in. If it includes a beer."

"Wouldn't be lunch without beer. Or dinner without whiskey. I know just the place." Ham and Eggs told him, starting to move to the door. The place turned out to be the Aspen Ridge Brewery where, thankfully, Cutter's cowgirl was not to be seen.

They were done with their sandwiches, drinking their third beer, talking about great golf courses they had played when Ruth Roberts reached Mayor Humphrey on the phone.

"Yes, Ruth, what can I do for you?" Humphrey asked.

"I just need a comment from you on the new parks director," Ruth replied.

Silence. Finally Humphrey blurted, "What?" caught himself, and added, "Oh, I'm sure the parks commission has chosen a fine director. We haven't had a chance to meet yet, but hope to tomorrow." He was so angry his temples throbbed.

"Hey, as long as I have you on the phone and we're talking about parks, I heard a few months ago that you had some special interest in Riverside Park. Care to comment on that?" she asked.

He damned near dropped the phone. "Uh. Uh. No. Have no idea what you're talking about. I love all of our parks. Hey, unless you have something else, I'm really busy right now." He hung up without waiting for a response.

Ruth looked at her phone. Odd. Didn't know about the new director. Didn't like the Riverside Park question. What the hell was going on?

FOUR

At seven o'clock on Monday morning, Cutter met Hugh in front of the parks administration building in Chalk Creek Park, about a mile and a half west of City Hall. The building had at one time been an upscale lodge for hunters and fishermen but was converted to offices right after the citizens of Columbus wrested control of the parks away from the politicians. The building was old but well cared for and had a distinctive Old West feel. Cutter loved it immediately. Hugh brought Cutter a set of master keys, but they found the office already open and lit up. Cutter's inherited assistant was already at her desk and the coffee was made. He decided on the spot he liked her.

Alicia Lein had worked for the department for over twenty-five years. Cutter would be her fourth director. When her husband called her to the television the morning before to watch the surprise announcement of the new director, Alicia had gone to work. Literally. She had dragged her husband away from his plan to watch an early season Rockies game to help her get the office ready. Over the next five hours, she 1) researched the internet for everything she could find on Winston Williams (which was not much, though his wife seemed to be a big shot); 2) assembled current project files for him to review; 3) set out an organization chart and personnel files for top staff; and 4) cleaned out all remaining traces of the now incarcerated Bob Wayne.

After Hugh introduced Cutter to Alicia, she summarily dismissed him, saying, "Thank you so much for bringing Director Williams in, Mr. Stalter, but I think he and I can handle it from here." Hugh knew when he was no longer needed. Alicia was now in charge.

"So, Alicia, or should I call you Ms. Lein?"

"Alicia is just fine. Just don't shorten it to Alice, okay?"

"Okay. Please call me Cutter."

"Yes sir. Except when others are around. I would prefer to use Director or Director Williams then, if that is alright." Reminding others that she worked for The Director was important to her. Solidified her position in the feeding chain. "I have arranged for you to meet all the administrative staff in your office at ten. That's about a dozen people. I sent them an email this morning."

"Unsend it."

"What? But I assumed you would want to meet your staff right away. This is kind of sudden and they might want to meet with you before they talk with their staffs."

Cutter put up his hand. "I have another idea." Alicia looked skeptical. "I would like you to set up back-to-back meetings at one and two. A half hour each. All staff. They can come whichever time they wish, but I do not want to close any offices or facilities. Attendance mandatory for everyone. Tell folks there will be a test afterwards."

"Really?"

"No. But you don't need to share that." He finally got her to smile. "Beforehand, I want you to walk me through these piles of files, you know, give me the short version of the projects and what you think of the people. And I want an hour with Bob Cratchit."

Alicia turned her head to the side and down. Looked like a chicken trying to decide if a spot was a bug or a rock. "Who, sir?"

"Cratchit. The person in charge of keeping our books. We have one of those, don't we?"

"Oh. Oh, yessir, we do. Now I get it," though her face indicated she failed to see the humor. "That would be Rachel Red Cloud. She is our CFO."

"She any good?" Cutter wanted to know.

Alicia smiled again. "Well, she has more than a few scalps on her office totem pole." Alicia's smile disappeared abruptly. "I'm sorry sir. That's an inside joke between Rachel and me. Highly inappropriate. Please forgive me."

"That's okay. You'll find I have a real problem with being appropriate. I'm sure I'll embarrass you soon enough."

Alicia continued, "I should warn you, though, that Rachel feels personally responsible for what happened with our former director. Like she should have been aware of what was going on. Had more checks and balances in place. Nobody else blames her, but she blames herself."

"So let's us three start at eight-thirty, here."

"What if other staff want to meet you? Or have an appointment?"

"Alicia, at exactly eight, I am going to walk through the office and introduce myself to the folks here. If they are here, they'll meet me. If not, they can wait 'til later. Much later." Again Alicia smiled.

At eight, Cutter walked through the office, met each person there, which turned out to be less than half the people who worked there. By the time the rest bothered to show up, Cutter, Alicia and Rachel were behind closed doors. Where they remained until Cutter marched them out of the office at eleven-thirty to take them to lunch. He had two new female loves in his life. Though he was reserved about Rachel. In addition to being an accountant who had double majored in economics and accounting and who seemed to know where every department penny was, Rachel Red Cloud was take-your-breath-away gorgeous. He just hoped Sandy would let him keep her.

At eleven Alicia had taken an urgent call from the mayor's office. The mayor wanted Director Williams in his office at one-thirty. Alicia told the mayor's secretary okay and then told Cutter, "We'll have to change the time of the employee meetings. The mayor wants to see you at one-thirty in his office."

Cutter looked grim. Christ in a handbasket. Looked at Rachel, who shrugged her shoulders. Damn. Nope. He was hired to run this department and he worked for a commission. The mayor would have to wait. "Call them back. Tell them I am tied up with employees until five. If he wants, I'll buy him a beer then."

"Really? You really want me to say that?" Alicia asked.

"I do." So she did. And could not believe it when she not only got no push back, but the mayor's staff also agreed to the five o'clock beer. Damn, this guy had some kahunas. Or was very, very stupid. Best to tread lightly for a while.

At one o'clock, Cutter sat on a table on the stage of Bald Mountain Recreation Center, waiting for people to file in. Front and center sat Alicia and Rachel, both smiling. Cutter wanted to talk to all employees at the same time. He had learned over the years the best way to be misunderstood by employees was to have the chain of command pass the word down. Every organization was like a huge kindergarten playing the telephone message game. The information that went in one end never resembled the information that came out the other. And he had done this countless times. Only this time it was with an organization he was responsible for. Time to fish or cut bait. Which reminded him of a Cutter naming story and made him smile.

The aw-shucks Cutter stood up. He welcomed everyone, introduced himself, including his preference for the name Cutter and asked them to take out a pen and paper or notepad or cell phone to make notes with. Waited for the confusion and scurrying to subside.

"Okay. Are we ready? Over the next weeks and months we will all get to know each other, but I want to start today with my rules. Few. Simple. Easy to remember. Easy to follow. Absolute. Second chances are hard to earn. Easier to just follow the rules.

"When I was a kid, my parents decided that with eight children, it was way too difficult to constantly be refereeing or negotiating or giving out hundreds of lessons. They gave my brothers and sisters and me seven rules. You only have to remember six of them. Write these down and memorize them. From time to time, I may hold up from one to six fingers and you need to repeat the rule back to me. Everybody understand?"

His audience either nodded or sat still, unsmiling.

"One. Don't get hurt. Two. Don't forget the first rule. Three. Take care of your coworkers. Four. Treat other people like you want to be treated. Five. The most important rule. Have fun. Six. Don't take things that don't belong to you. Simple. Right? I'll repeat them to make sure you got them down right." And he did.

He continued, "Just three more things to write down. Not rules so much as ways to do business. First, if you tell someone you will do something, you are responsible for getting it done. Not your coworker, not your supervisor. You. Don't promise something unless you personally can make it happen. Second, never, under any circumstances, should you lie to the press. That does not mean you have to tell them everything you know. And unless you know it for a fact, don't share what you think might be. The press is not a court of law. A perfectly fine response to the question 'Do you still beat your wife, yes or no?' is 'I have always been kind to my mother'."

Finally something he said brought a reaction from the crowd of employees. Some laughter.

"Third, you are not allowed to say 'no' to our customers. If you can't find a way to say 'yes', turn them over to your supervisor. If the supervisor can't find a way to say 'yes', send it up the chain." This final one got reaction of outright bewilderment. Lots of "huhs" and "whats" and "is he kiddings?"

"Okay. Anyone need anything repeated? No? Great. If you will all just stay seated for a minute, I'm going to go back to the exit door so we can shake hands as you leave. Tell me your name and where you work. I won't remember the first time, but eventually I'll get it. And thanks for coming in."

At two o'clock, with Alicia and Rachel still down front, he repeated the performance, with pretty much the same reaction. Afterwards, he met with the rest of the administrative team: two assistant directors, the head of maintenance and construction, the chief planner, the human resources manager, the head of public information and fund raising and the special projects manager. None seemed happy for him to be there. Especially after he had talked directly to all of their employees. Without consulting them first. Christ in a handbasket. This was going to be a battle.

A few minutes before five, Cutter drove to City Hall where his city car was waved into the building's underground parking garage. Instead of going straight over to the elevator, he walked back out to the parking attendant and introduced himself. The attendant, whose nametag said "Hi! I'm Chuck," looked shocked that someone, especially a director, would come to see him. Cutter had learned long ago that assistants, clerks and parking attendants made you or broke you. You could never have too many on your side.

"Hi, Chuck. I'm Cutter Williams. I just started at the Parks and Recreation Department. Just wanted to say hi and thank you for finding me a space."

Chuck beamed. "Oh, sure. No problem. Anytime." Before he could ask how Cutter knew his name, Cutter trotted away.

The receptionist in Mayor Humphrey's office kept him waiting for twenty minutes. He was not surprised. He used the time to peruse the walls, which were covered with photographs of the mayor with the governor and the vice president and a myriad of other dignitaries. The picture center stage was one of a much younger mayor shaking hands with Bob Redford, both of them in ski clothes. At that time, Carleton Humphrey looked like he might actually be able to ski down a mountain. Now he looked like he would just roll down. Fat, short, bald, florid, with jowls a bulldog would envy.

"Mr. Williams, nice to meet you." The mayor walked briskly out of his office toward Cutter, hand out. "I'm so sorry I wasn't able to greet you when you first got to town. The parks commission seems to have a problem with me, though I sure don't know why. I am one of Parks and Recreation's biggest supporters. But they didn't see fit to tell me you had been hired so I couldn't give you a proper welcome." Cutter noted that the mayor had used the old politician's trick of getting his practiced speech out without giving the other guy a chance to say anything.

"Nice to meet you, Mr. Mayor. And I apologize for not coming to see you first thing this morning. I so appreciate your making time for me now in your busy schedule. How about I buy you a beer? Pick your brain a little? I'm sure you have lots to share with me." Right back atcha, Your Honor.

"Fine. Fine. Be right with you." With that the mayor turned to the receptionist, harrumphed a couple of do this's and that's, and told her he was leaving for the evening. Humphrey led the way out of the office and down onto the street. "Morgan House okay?"

"Whatever you choose is fine," Cutter answered. The Morgan House was an old hotel converted to a bar and restaurant on the first floor and upscale condos on the upper floors. Condos mostly owned by skiers who left them empty forty-eight weeks a year. The bar seemed to be the meeting place for the public officials and those who wanted something from the public officials. Humphrey even had his own table in the back corner of the room; his seat in the corner where he could survey the entire place without turning his head. It took them five minutes to get to the table after they entered since the mayor had to stop and chat with everyone on the way in. Important man. Highly sought after. Busy, busy. Introduced Cutter to everyone as "my new parks director."

After they were finally seated and drinks ordered, the mayor started in, "Well, Son, tell me about yourself. Where are you from? How is it that the commission picked you? Where else have you been parks director? Married? Family?" His Honor was a font of questions. Cutter felt like the only things missing were a bare light bulb and a rubber hose.

Cutter thought for a moment—the long answers or the short ones? Opted for the very short, "Not much to tell. Davenport, Iowa. I don't know. Nowhere. Yes. Yes." Gave the mayor his aw-shucks grin.

Carleton looked at him, confusion clouding his eyes. "What?"

"You asked me six questions which I answered." Confusion was replaced by irritation. Bingo.

Carleton tried again, "So you were parks director in Davenport?"

Cutter backed off. "No. I have never been a parks director. In fact, I have never worked in parks and recreation."

"I don't understand. Why would they hire you if you know nothing about parks? Sometimes I think those commissioners do things just to try to make me look bad."

Cutter realized he might just be exacerbating a problem, not helping solve it. "I'm sorry, Mayor. They didn't hire me for my knowledge of parks and recreation. My area of expertise, if I have one, is helping fix broken organizations. I think the commission was looking for someone to right the ship that Director Wayne had steered into the rocks." He didn't feel the need to add his primary objective of keeping the parks out of the mayor's hands.

The mayor's smile returned, "Oh. I see. Well, that makes perfect sense. I understand now." What he didn't feel the need to share was that while having his own guy in charge of parks would be best, second best might just be having a director who knew nothing about parks. This might just all work out fine.

Cutter drank his beer and the mayor his bourbon and branch water. They talked about the city, about Sandy and Jordan and the baby on the way, about the best places to look for a house, about local beers and about the Cubs and the Rockies and which team was worse. Folks drifted to and from the table, looking to curry the mayor's favor. Ninety minutes after they sat down, Carleton rose and excused himself. Had an important dinner to get to. Thanked Cutter for the drink. Invited him to sit on his cabinet and told him cabinet meeting was the next day at nine. Stopped at almost every table on the way out.

Cutter was watching the mayor work the room, again, when Ruth Roberts plopped down in the chair just vacated by His Honor. Cutter used his Judy Garland/Dorothy Gale voice, "My! People come and go so quickly here."

Ruth was so intense she didn't notice. She was already in ace reporter mode. "I'm Ruth Roberts with the *Columbus City Times*. Aren't you Winston Williams, the new parks director?"

"What's left of him."

"I…What? What do you mean, what's left of him?"

"I go by Cutter. What can I do for you?"

Ruth was not used to being on the defensive. "How do you like our mayor?"

"I like him fine."

"So you'll be able to work with him okay?"

"I see no reason why not."

Ruth said nothing, the reporter trick to get someone to volunteer more information. Cutter just smiled and waited. Finally she asked, "Did the mayor ask you anything about Riverside Park?"

"No."

She waited. Still Cutter volunteered nothing.

"You don't talk much, do you?"

"On the contrary. My wife says I talk too much." Ruth gave up and excused herself. Again Cutter said, "My! People come and go so quickly here," this time to himself.

FIVE

Cutter waited as patiently as he could as Sandy and Jordan came up the gate ramp at Chaffee County International Airport. When Jordan saw him, she squealed and ran to him, jumping up into his arms to hug him. Sandy approached, all smiles. Smiles until Cutter said, in his loud trying-to-embarrass-you voice, "Oh My God! You're pregnant! What have you been doing while I was here?"

Equally loud, "A girl has to have her needs taken care of. You run off and, well, my trainer, he stayed around," her smile returning. She hugged him and very quietly whispered into his ear, "I have missed you so much."

"Daddy, can we go ride a horse?"

"You betcha, Shortcakes."

"Right now? I wore my new cowgirl boots, see?" Jordan pulled up the legs of her jeans to show Cutter her bright red cowgirl boots.

"Wow! Those are pretty nice boots you got there, Pardner. Maybe we can find a red horse to go with them."

"Really, Daddy? With a red saddle too?"

"We'll see what we can find," Cutter promised.

"Can you let go of me now so I can breathe," Sandy

asked. Cutter didn't realize he had been squeezing her the entire time. "So how's it going, big fella? Got the job under control? Found us a house yet?"

"Actually I have found a place for you to look at. East side of Riverside Park. I thought we could drive by on the way to the hotel. I hope you like it. I'm real tired of living in the hotel, having a maid clean up after me every day, having to eat in a restaurant every day, having a bar in my basement that stays open until one every day. I tell you, it's been a burden."

Cutter had been in Columbus for four weeks, and this was the only time they could come visit him before Junior was due in July. They had decided the move would wait until right before school. Jerry Randolph, who was paying Sandy the consulting fee through the Arts Council, wasn't too happy about his consultant being so far away until then, but since Cutter seemed to be faring well and the parks were still afloat, he didn't whine too much. Sandy was going to spend a couple of days in the office this week before she returned to Iowa.

As they drove to check out the house, Jordan piped up from the back seat, "Hey, Daddy, guess what? Mom said when she gets the new baby, I can get a dog. I'm going to name him Baily and feed him and walk him and play with him and everything!" Cutter shot Sandy a less than happy look.

Under his breath, "Terrific. That'll last about two days and then guess who gets to take care of the damn thing." Louder, "Gee that's great, Shortcakes."

Again from the back seat, "Hey Mom, since you get a new baby and I get a new dog, can Daddy get a pet too?"

Sandy smiled and told her, "Sure, honey. Your daddy can get a pet chicken," and she poked Cutter in the ribs. He finally smiled back.

Sandy loved the house. Lots of wood, lots of windows, lots of great views of the mountains. Big stone fireplace and a deck. Two blocks east of Riverside Park, on a cul-de-sac off Brown's Canyon Road. She noted it overlooked a golf course several blocks to the south. How handy for Cutter. "So, Mr. Director, how much are they asking?" Cutter told her and she raised her eyebrows, almost to her hairline. "Pretty pricey, don't you think?"

Dorothy Gale reappeared with "Well, we're not in Kansas anymore, Toto. Or Iowa for that matter. But from what I've seen, it's a good deal. We can look cheaper. Up to you." He tried to affect an I-don't-really-care attitude, but she saw right through it...subtle was not Cutter's strong point. She relented.

"We'll let Jordan decide," she told him. Jordan was already picking out her room and deciding where Baily would sleep.

"Hey, Shortcakes, you want to live here?"

"Yes, Daddy. Can we keep a horse in the backyard?"

"I don't think so, but there is a stable in Riverside Park, right over there," pointing through the window toward Riverside Park, "and they have lots of horses to ride."

Sandy told him, "Call the realtor." Cutter had his cell phone out dialing before she got to realtor. Made an offer.

They spent the rest of the day exploring the city, with time set aside for Sandy to get a long nap. Which was pregnantspeak for time away from Jordan. They had dinner at a traditional western steakhouse, where Jordan and the server admired each other's red cowgirl boots. Just as dessert arrived the realtor called with a counter offer which they accepted.

Jordan was so tuckered out, (one of Cutter's new Western words which irritated the shit out of Sandy), she fell asleep on Cutter's shoulder before they made it to the car. After they got her tucked safely into bed, Cutter raided the room's mini bar, an airplane gin and tonic for him and straight tonic for Sandy. She eyed the small bottles of wine in the bar and growled at him. Told him the next time, if there was a next time, he got to carry the baby and give up drinking, just to see how he liked it. They climbed into the bed and as consolation, he rubbed her feet. It only slightly mollified her.

"Tell me about the job. Is this going to work out, or should we pull the plug before I pack up and leave Iowa?" she wanted to know.

"I'll tell you," he started, "this place could be a case study in how you use government to fuck up paradise." Sandy raised her eyebrows, kissed him on the cheek to divert his attention, and stole a big swallow of his gin. He pretended he didn't notice. "My second day on the job, I attended a mayor's cabinet meeting. In all our time helping organizations, I have never, and I mean never, seen anything like it. Carleton Humphrey is a bona fide lunatic. He meets with his staff, the directors, the assistant directors, the city attorney and city auditor, the assistant assistant directors and several others I can't identify, some forty-five people in one room. He rolls out a file cabinet on wheels and goes through forty-five files, one for each person in the room. In each file are the memos, letters and orders he has sent the person, and he asks for an update on each item. If he doesn't like the update, he yells at them or belittles them or threatens to fire them.

"This meeting lasts between three and four hours. I sat there and figured out that with the money wasted by all those high priced people sitting there being miserable, I could run a playground for seven years. And that's each meeting. Pure fucking agony. I figured that maybe this was a once a month or once a quarter exercise. I went back the next week. Same room. Same people. Same file cabinet. Same stupid memos, same stupid threats from hizzoner. I can't believe they don't, at the least, walk out *en masse*. Or stage a violent coup.

"I haven't been back. Humphrey called me and ordered me to attend. Said my absence was demoralizing to the rest of the team. Called Hugh and ordered him to order me to attend."

"What did you do?" Sandy asked, though she knew what the answer was.

"Bet you think I told him to fuck off, don't you?"

"Uh huh."

"I didn't. I told him the parks department was so screwed up, I couldn't afford to spend four hours a week listening to other people's problems, but that I would be more than happy to spend an hour with him each week briefing him on our progress, keeping him in the loop."

"And?"

"What choice did he have? He told me I'd be sorry, but he took my offer. Now we meet at five-thirty on Mondays and I buy his bourbons. Makes him feel less like a loser."

"You're a peach, Cutter. What can I say? How about council?"

"Much better. They actually know what they're doing. Organized, thoughtful and they don't dawdle. Ninety-nine percent of the legislation goes through without much discussion. If there is opposition, speakers are limited to three for and three against and each speaker has three minutes. All quite civilized. And since we aren't under the mayor, council considers parks as their special purview. I'm the new golden child." Cutter grinned.

"And your staff?" Sandy wondered, but she was stifling a yawn, not out of boredom, but fatigue.

"You'll see when you work with them. For the most part, a good bunch, but they are so used to being treated as the poor stepchild, they are negative and everything is 'woe is me'. The finance officer is top notch—you'll undoubtedly glom onto her—and the planning guy is

54

sharp, but will have to be pried open to new ideas. To him, if you aren't a landscape architect, you can't possibly know anything about how to design a park. He and I will either come to terms, or we might have to find him a new challenge..." Cutter quit talking. Sandy had started to snore.

The next morning, Cutter left early for work and Sandy took Jordan to the Board of Education administration building and registered her for school. Afterwards, they stopped to visit Cutter at his office, met some of the parks staff and made plans for dinner. By two o'clock, the girls had explored their new neighborhood and revisited the house where Sandy took measurements and worked out what furniture would be moved and what new things she would get to buy. She felt the nesting urge kick into full gear and grinned as she made a list of purchases to be made. Decided this move was going to be a lot more fun than she had thought.

At the same time Sandy was deciding to scrap all of their living room furniture (except for Cutter's monster television) and replace it with overstuffed leather and varnished wood, Ruth Robert's cell phone rang. Even though she was in the middle of an interview with a local judge about his drinking habits, and even though a bead of sweat had appeared on the judge's forehead, she excused herself to take the call. She knew better than to let Ty Carroll go to voice mail.

"Mr. Carroll, sir. How can I help you?" she asked.

"Ruth, I need you to do me a little favor," Ty said

softly. "When you get a little time, could you check out the new parks director? You know, just background stuff. Make a few calls; talk to people he used to work with. You don't need to talk to him or anyone here locally. Not yet, anyway. This isn't for an article but send me your report when you finish. No hurry. When you get to it."

"Yessir, you bet." Ruth understood the code words. No hurry was Tyspeak for right fucking now. No article meant this was for Ty's eyes only. Just background stuff meant find any dirt you can. But Ruth was still a reporter and without thinking she asked, "Does this have anything to do with Riverside Park?"

Ty waited long enough to reply that Ruth developed a bead of sweat of her own. "Why would you ask that, Ruth?" Ty finally answered, a glint of gunfighter in his voice. Ruth felt like there was a hand wrapped around her throat and she couldn't choke out a response. Ty went on, "I'm not interested in Riverside Park, just the director. Understood?"

"Perfectly, Sir," she managed to get out. But Ty had already hung up. She stared at the phone for a full minute before the judge asked if there was anything else. Ruth looked at him as if he had appeared from nowhere. She said, "No. Nothing else," and waved him away. By the time he had retreated twenty feet, he was on his phone, arranging to take a leave of absence and to do a stint in rehab. Quietly thanking whoever had called Ruth and put her off the track.

The following morning, as Ruth immersed herself in finding everything she could about Winston Weller Williams, Cutter was dropping Jordan off at one of his department's summer camps where she could learn about horses and actually ride a horse. After Jordan assured him, "Daddy, I'll be fine. I've watched lots of shows about riding horses and I know how to do it," Cutter warned her for the umpteenth time to be careful, and he left her to meet Sandy at his office.

Cutter was having a difficult time wrapping his head around city financing and his budget. Based on the expertise he had shown handling his own finances, Sandy was not surprised and decided that would be a good place to start working. She had the rare talent of not only grasping the subtleties of government funding, but also the ability to translate figures on a page into workable programs. She spent the morning being briefed by Rachel on the budgets, both operations and capital. The capital budget was straightforward. Council had provided some funds to both expand the park system and to do some renovations. Council members realized in Columbus nothing garnered votes like a new park.

The operating budget seemed frugal, especially for a city which was in good financial shape and appeared to value its parks. Sandy asked Rachel, "So what's the story with this operating budget? Is it a tight year for the city?"

Rachel raised her eyebrows. "No. Hefty increase city wide, but ours is the same as last year. Same thing has been happening for several years. Been that way through our last two directors."

"Why is that?" Sandy asked.

"I don't know. We always had plenty of money while Director Bryce was here." Tom Bryce had been director for fifteen years and was a local legend. Popular with the public, popular with the press, envied by the politicians. Even had a park named after him. Rachel went on, "After Bryce retired, the commission was not happy with the internal candidates and thought the department needed some new blood. They hired a woman, Theresa Blackman, who had been director in a couple of cities in Ohio. It took her two years to parlay this job into one in Denver, where they finally figured out she was just a talking head and sent her packing. But the budget started to decline when she was here.

"The commission decided to go back to promoting from within. Director Wayne was, frankly, not up to the job. When his first proposed budget was submitted, the mayor's office cut it to shreds. I gave him all the ammunition he needed to make our case to council, even wrote his comments for his budget presentation. Demonstrated how the parks budget had declined while internal support budgets like finance and the mayor's office had doubled. Director Wayne decided not to fight. In hindsight, it looks like he didn't want anyone looking too closely at where his budget money was going. That year, or the next three."

Sandy wanted to know, "Do you still have those comments?"

"I do," Rachel replied, smiling. "And even though it was a fruitless exercise I updated them every year. You want to see them?"

"That'd be great. Thanks."

At dinner, Jordan could not stop talking about horse camp, how she had gotten to ride a horse and everything. Though she complained that her teacher wouldn't let her hold the reins and she wasn't allowed to gallop. And she didn't like the way the horse smelled. When her ice cream showed up, she finally quit jabbering. Cutter asked Sandy how her time with Mrs. Red Cloud had gone.

"You were right. Rachel is one smart lady. I'm surprised the commission didn't consider her for the job. You should be hearing footsteps and watching over your shoulder," Sandy said and then paused, thinking about what she had just said. "On second thought, you should not be looking at her at all. I'm all fat and bloated and ugly and she's a knockout." Cutter grinned, until he saw that Sandy was serious.

"Babe, you are gorgeous. Beautiful beyond description."

Sandy harrumphed but went on, "At any rate, Rachel gave me plenty to work on. I'm taking the budgets for the last ten years home with me to see what we can do. You need to make nice with the mayor and the finance director. And the council. Especially the council."

"You got it. What else, boss?"

"Get your planning guy to sit down with your maintenance guy to go over all the improvements scheduled for the next three years, so maintenance can come up with budget needs as new things come on line. And have someone work on program trends to determine what needs to go and what needs to be increased. They haven't done anything new for the last eight years."

"Is that all?" a bit of irritation in Cutter's voice.

"Nope. We need to come up with something for these people to work towards. It all feels stagnant."

"And?" Cutter now sounded pissed.

"Take us back to the hotel. And rub my feet. Jordan and I are going shopping tomorrow."

Cutter finally smiled.

SIX

Two weeks later, Cutter had fallen asleep watching an old movie when his cell phone buzzed. He had been revisiting an old nightmare and was slow to answer, and when he did it was with, "Christ in a handbasket. What?" Cringed when he realized what he'd said.

"I catch you at a bad time?" Cutter couldn't place the voice.

"No. Sorry. I was asleep."

"Oh, I'm sorry. Would another time be better?" Still no idea who was on the phone.

"No. No. I must have dozed off. What can I do for you?"

"Play golf with me. Someone I want you to meet and get to know. Thursday afternoon. Kyvtop Country Club. My treat. Well, not exactly my treat. Guest of a friend of mine. Cocktails after. Loser's treat." Finally Cutter figured out the caller from the staccato delivery. Council President Eggleston.

"I'd love to, Mr. President."

"Ham and Eggs, Son. Ham and Eggs. Call me Ham and Eggs," Hammond said. "Great. We're guests of Cord Richards, a guy you need to know. Executive assistant to the publisher of the paper, Mr. Carroll. Good guy. Cord. Not Carroll. Well, Carroll's okay, just not my kind of guy. I'll drive. Pick you up at your office at noon?"

Took Cutter a few seconds to realize Ham and Eggs was waiting for a response. "Sure, that would be great, sir."

"See you then. Bring your A game. You'll need it," and Ham and Eggs hung up.

Kyvtop. The best the state had to offer. Very exclusive. Hosted a PGA tourney for a few years, until the young players, new equipment and no way to push the tee boxes back eliminated it from the tour. Cutter could spend time working on his relationship with council. Get to meet the most powerful man in the city's number two. Cutter was beginning to love this job.

At twenty before noon on Thursday, Ham and Eggs bounced into Cutter's office. "Sorry to intrude. Okay if I walk around the office and say hi to folks? Your predecessor didn't like politicians mingling with his people. Thought I should check with you."

"No problem, sir. Please do. I think they generally feel left out so that would be great," Cutter told him. Ham and Eggs whirled around and was gone. Half an hour later, Ham and Eggs bounced back in.

"Come on, Son. We're late. Wonderful staff you have here. Nice people. Hard at work. Seemed shocked to see me. Shook some hands, patted some backs. Maybe won a vote or two." He was gone as quickly as he arrived. Cutter told Alicia he was leaving and walked to his car where Eggleston was waiting. He loaded his clubs and shoes and Ham and Eggs squealed his tires as he pulled out of the parking lot. Twenty minutes later they were at Kyvtop where staff unloaded their clubs and directed them to the clubhouse locker room.

Cutter had a difficult time not gaping like a rube when he entered the locker room. Thirty foot ceiling, all wood with a stone fireplace covering a whole wall. Big enough to roast a whole deer in. Two deer. Maybe even two deer and a boar. A few guys walking around, some in towels. Five ancient men playing poker, two of them bare-assed naked. They had been handed keys to their lockers, and Cutter looked around but didn't see any sign of lockers. Just before he made a complete ass of himself by asking where they were, he realized the wood paneling on the walls were actually locker doors. Cutter had played some nice courses before but this intimidated him.

Eggleston had already stripped to his underwear and Cutter was shocked to see how skinny he looked, all bones and dark skin. Wondered how he could even swing a club, let alone hit a ball more than a hundred yards. Ham and Eggs was donning a golf outfit that would have stood out even in Miami. Bright mint green from head to toe, socks included, with a white belt and white shoes. Cutter was marveling at all of it when someone tapped him on the shoulder. He turned and was greeted by a huge smile beneath a Wild Bill Hickok mustache and steel gray eyes.

"Mr. Williams," Wild Bill said, "I'm Cord Richards. Glad you could join us today. I've heard good things about you."

"Nice to meet you," Cutter said, offering his hand. "Thank you for inviting me. And please, call me Cutter." Wondered how it was that Richards had heard about him. Of course, Cutter had no way of knowing about the Ruth Roberts report which Ty had shared with Cord. Her report was one thing that led to this invitation. Since Ruth had found pretty much the same things the parks commission had found, Ty and Cord had the same reaction. This Williams guy might be a flake, might be sharp. Ruth had discovered one thing the commission had not—that Cutter had been treated for anxiety and severe depression, though she could not determine what led to his "breakdown."

"Hey, Ham and Eggs, how's it going?" Cord greeted the council president.

"Great. Fine. Perfect day for golf. Thanks for inviting us. Good to be back."

"Soon as you two are suited up, meet me in the club room. We'll grab a beer and a sandwich and go hit a few balls. Not many players out today, so we can tee off when we're ready," Cord said over his shoulder as he was leaving.

"Not many players" was an understatement. From what Cutter could see from the terrace where they were finishing their beers, there was not a soul on the course. When Cutter asked why, Ham and Eggs explained the history of the club. On a trip back east, Kit Junior had met Walter Hagen at a party, or more precisely a Bacchanalia, where Hagen was holding court. Seeing that

64

they shared a common interest in all things hedonistic, they hit it off. Hagen convinced Kit Junior that golf was a game for the rich, for those who wanted to rub elbows with the rich and for those who wanted to separate the rich from some of their riches, Hagen's personal specialty. Kit Junior came back to Columbus and built its first golf course. Hagen was right. But by the time Arnold Palmer came along, golf had become the purview of the masses, leaving the rich no place to congregate apart from that crowd.

Ty's father loved the game, almost as much as he hated the common rabble, so he gathered a hundred of his closest friends together and they built Kyvtop. Took the name "kyv" from the Ute word for "mountain". Native Americans in the area took it as an insult, but the founders didn't care. They made it exclusive. Very exclusive. There was no membership application, no waiting list to join. Two ways a person could get in: inherit a membership or be asked. No one ever turned down an invitation. Until the nineties, no women were allowed on the course, but finally the club bowed to pressure and invited a few women and minorities to join. Only about one hundred twenty members today. There were no fees. At the end of the year, they took the costs of operating the club, divided it by the number of members and sent out a bill. Anyone didn't pay, they were banned for life.

"Ham and Eggs makes it sound pretty snooty," Cord contended. "It isn't really. Just a bunch of folks who really love the game."

65

"Yeah. Just regular people. Who happen to be rich. Like Hemingway told Fitzgerald," Ham and Eggs countered, but good-naturedly. "So we gonna gab or play golf?" With that, he jumped from his chair and was down the steps before Cord could respond. Cord laughed, shook his head and followed him down the steps. Cutter hurried to catch up.

The first hole was a medium length par five, slightly uphill. Ham and Eggs teed off first. He had a slow precise swing, the most graceful Cutter had ever seen. Two hundred fifty yards, slight draw, to the middle of the fairway. Cutter wondered how such a scrawny little body could hit it so far. For the second time that day, he was intimidated. He and Cord teed off and neither came close to Ham and Egg's ball. Cord suggested Cutter ride with him, since it was obvious they were going to play catch up all day.

By the sixth hole, Cutter was in awe. Every lie was above or below his feet, or uphill or downhill, or some combination thereof. The course was beautiful, the holes brilliantly designed. The greens were perfectly manicured, fast but fair. He wished, not for the first time, he had been born rich. He was self-aware enough to understand he didn't have the drive to make himself rich, but still. He was enjoying the game, the scenery and mostly the company. Cord, it turned out, was the ideal golfing companion. They traded jokes, stories and "good shots" as they rode together. Ham and Eggs was strangely quiet, but then he was already two under par and intensely into the game. Cord was four over and Cutter eight over, so it was obvious who would be buying those post round drinks. Cutter didn't care.

"Ham and Eggs is kind of a strange guy," Cutter said to Cord. "What's his story?"

Cord chuckled and told Cutter what he knew. Eggleston was about sixty, as near as anyone could determine. He had arrived in Columbus some thirty years ago. Got a job as a community affairs manager with the board of education. He'd landed the job, according to the local pundits, on the basis of his skin color and his affability. He threw his boundless energy into working with community groups, helping them get set up and organized, raising money for them, interceding for them if need be. He made a few enemies along the way, but made a lot more friends. He never passed up an opportunity to attend social events where he could meet the movers and shakers of the city. Eventually, a bank, the one owned by the Carroll family, found themselves in trouble because of their lending practices in the minority community. The bank offered him a vice presidency to handle community affairs for them. He got the bank through the turmoil.

He married a white woman slightly older than he was, which made him a few more enemies. They got divorced, and he earned a few more. His wife's brother, Carleton Humphrey, moved to the top of Ham and Egg's enemy list. Cart, as Eggleston called him, was by that time on City Council. He had been an assistant football coach at the university, a job he lost because his coaching style was over the top. He had offered players incentives to hurt opposing players, not exactly a sporting tactic. He couldn't find another job, so he decided to run for City Council. He ran on a bombastic platform. According to his campaign speeches, which he delivered with ardent fervor, every elected official was on the take and every civil servant was a lazy idler. The people ate that shit up. He was elected and continued his ranting and raving. It wasn't productive, but the voters began watching council on television just to follow his antics. Carleton used his bully pulpit to attack Eggleston and whatever issue Eggleston was supporting whenever the occasion presented itself.

In order to level the playing field, Ty Carroll went to see Ham and Eggs to ask him to run for council. Ham and Eggs wasn't wild about the idea, but since his boss of bosses asked, he agreed. Which led to an unexpected problem. Of course, Ty's paper and his media outlets supported his candidacy, but an opposing television station decided to investigate Eggleston's background. They discovered he had spent six months in jail in Memphis on a misdemeanor charge. Ham and Eggs had gone into the wrong bar and some local white trash boys decided to have some fun with the "little half-breed shithead." Ham and Eggs busted a beer bottle over the leader's head and hurt him badly enough the guy ended up in the hospital. But not until after Eggleston had taken a severe beating and gotten arrested and thrown in jail.

Under state law, the misdemeanor barred Ham and Eggs from running for public office. He went to tell Ty he was withdrawing from the race, but Ty was hearing none of it. Ty was pissed and told him "No fucking way you are quitting. We can fix this little hiccup." Ty did exactly that. Used his contacts to have Eggleston's record expunged. Humphrey went on the attack, but Ham and Eggs won easily. Eventually Humphrey was elected mayor and Eggleston became president of council. Their animosity never waned. Ty supported both; he liked the balance it gave to city politics.

Cord ended the story as he stood over a twenty foot putt on the sixteenth hole. He looked up at Cutter and said, "Ham and Eggs is one of my favorite people. Big heart, small ego. The exact opposite of Humphrey." He smiled and rolled in the putt.

The course had continually risen uphill and the final tee box was on a promontory overlooking both the entire valley and the last fairway 200 yards below. It reminded Cutter of a course he had played in Granville, Ohio, but this was even more glorious. They all stood and admired the view until Ham and Eggs said, "Hear that, boys? That's a beer calling my name." Aided by the topography, he hit the longest drive of the day.

Thirty minutes later, they were on the terrace enjoying the Cutter-supplied drinks. They replayed the round, including Ham and Eggs' four-under performance and Cutter's four balls into the same pond on the short par three. As they finished their first cocktail, Ham and Eggs jumped up and said to Cutter, "C'mon, boy. We gotta go. I have a community meeting I have to attend."

Cutter rose and asked, "Anything I should go to?"

"Only if you're into laying sewer pipe," he laughed.

Cord called after his retreating golf partners, "Hey, Cutter, if you want to hang around and have a couple more drinks, I'll take you home."

Cutter hesitated and looked at Ham and Eggs who said, "No problem for me if you want to stay. Enjoy yourself. Call me tomorrow. Few things to discuss." With that he was gone.

"Thanks, sir," Cutter said to the space where Ham and Eggs had been.

Cord and Cutter ordered another round, Cutter telling the bartender, "Just a beer," and getting a really nice lager without having to answer twenty questions. This was a life he could live, he decided. They settled back into their chairs on the terrace, quietly admiring the gray mountains and declining sun. After five minutes of silence, Cord asked, "So you know Ham and Eggs story. What's yours? How did you get the name Cutter?"

Cutter smiled. "Everyone asks the same thing. I never thought it was strange, but people seem to think it must have some deep meaning. In fact, it's really stupid. When I was a little kid, I loved playing make-believe. Kinda sissy, eh? In fourth grade I finally got a chance to be in a school play. I thought I had died and gone to heaven. Our class was going to do *Alice in Wonderland* and I really wanted to be the Mad Hatter. But the only part they would give me was as a guard in the Queen of Hearts court. I had one line. I was one of three guards, the last one, who were supposed to say, 'Off with her head!' When the guards' time in the spotlight came, the first two guys did it perfectly, but I was really excited—my parents and sisters and brothers and friends were all there—so I yelled as loudly as possible, 'Cut her head off! Cut her head off!' The audience thought it was funny. The teacher, not so much. The next day in school, all of the rest of the cast started calling me 'Cut'er head off!' It caught on and was eventually shortened to 'Cutter'."

"Odd. I heard it had something to do with baseball," Cord said.

"Uhhh, there was that," Cutter replied.

"So what's the real story?"

"Actually, I have never told anyone the real story."

"Why not?"

"Because I have no fucking idea how I got the name. My family has always called me Cutter, and I like it a lot more than Winston." Cutter went on to tell the rest of his story. His family and schooling and his jump-around jobs, how he had ended up at Davenport City Hall, about Sandy and eventually getting married and about their work together. Cord laughed at the funny parts, asked questions about Davenport and wanted to know all about Sandy and Jordan and the kid on the way. Found out Jordan was the same age as his daughter and they would be going to the same school. Cord suggested they get some dinner. Told Cutter the club offered a great steak sandwich. They finished their meal and were on a second bottle of wine when Cutter asked about Cord's story.

"Not much to tell. I was a riverboat captain on the Mississippi for a while. Smuggled rum and ganja down

Martinique way. Fought the Apaches out in Arizona. You know, just ho-hum stuff. Nothing exciting like throwing chum off a fishing boat."

Cutter nodded his head knowingly. "I'm surprised. I had you pegged for being one of those fancy pants East Coast lawyers. Rags-to-riches story, Dickensesque orphan, raised by a kindly but quirky one-eyed shoemaker, worked at shoveling coal to put himself through college."

"Really? And here I grew this mustache just so you would buy the Indian fighter story."

"Well, Wild Bill, that does lend an air of authenticity to the claim," Cutter laughed.

The club manager came to tell them the dining room was closing down, but the bar was still open if they cared for another drink. They both cared deeply so they each got a drink and retired to the locker room where Cutter noticed the poker game was still in progress, but with new players. According to Cord the same game had been going on for over twenty years, players coming and going. After they claimed a spot by the fireplace, Cutter said, "So tell me more about fighting Apaches."

Cord shared his tale. The rags-to-riches guess by Cutter was closer than he thought. Cord Richards grew up in Waynesville, Ohio where he, his parents and two sisters lived in a small apartment above one of the twenty antique stores on Main Street. His dad worked for the maintenance department of the village, in fact was the only worker in the department and every night came home smelling of sewer and/or asphalt. He was a good dad, and although Cord and his sisters didn't have much, there was always plenty of food and clean clothes.

It was a small town life, full of small town adventures, people and prejudices. Cord always assumed he would work for the village like his dad when he got out of high school. Until a new kid, Chris Bugg, moved to town. Bugg's folks were well off, at least by Waynesville standards. Cord would go to Bugg's big house and think this is what I want when I grow up, not an apartment on Main Street. Chris talked about going off to college and being a lawyer, like his dad. Cord saw college as his way out. Problem was, they had no money and his grades weren't good enough to earn a scholarship. He played three sports in high school, all of them poorly.

Then he heard about ROTC. If a guy could pass the entrance exam and would sign up to do a four-year tour of duty after graduation, the army would send him to college. He took the exam, did well and four and a half years later he was a freshly minted United States Army lieutenant. Assigned to infantry, it was all pretty boring, right up to when war broke out. Within two months he was leading guard patrols and spending twenty-four hours a day worrying about dying. His patrol was caught in an ambush. He got all but one out safely. That one had done what Cord told him not to do, stuck his head up to look around. A sniper took the top of his head off. He died in Cord's arms, with Cord assuring him everything was going to be alright.

Cord left the army the day his enlistment was up. Got a job doing human resources for a chain of suburban newspapers in Cincinnati. Cord told people that calling human resources work boring was redundant. Then several things happened which made it a little more exciting. First, the reporters decided they would unionize. The company hired an outside negotiating team to fight the unionization. Cord was put on the team. Next, the night before the first set of negotiations, the head negotiator fell off the wagon. Hard. Cord was put in charge. He was nothing short of brilliant and settled the issue in the company's favor. Finally, he fell in love with one of his teammates, Beth Chamberlin, and they got married.

A couple of years later, when Ty Carroll went looking for someone to handle his union problems, he was directed to Cord. Hired him. For a very large salary. Within the first two years, Cord became Ty's favorite. Cord now had his own set of keys to the Carroll Kingdom.

Some of this Cutter had to pry out of Cord, urging the saga on with comments like, "So Wild Bill, how much did Ty offer you?" or "What did you do in the war?" By ten o'clock they knew more about each other in one day than most people knew about either of them in a year. It seemed natural to both of them.

Cord admitted to Cutter he was too drunk to drive but added the club had sleeping rooms, and they could stay there. By the time Cord returned from the manager's office with the room keys, Cutter was asleep in his chair.

SEVEN

"Cutter, the doctor says it's time for you to come home. Junior will be along any day now. So, big boy, get your ass in gear. Let me know what time your plane lands. Talk to you soon." Cutter listened to the voice mail a second time, grinning. Finally he was going to get to meet Junior. Seemed like it had been the longest nine months of his life. He called Hugh, Ham and Eggs and, purely as a courtesy, the mayor's office and told them he would be gone for a week or two. Twelve hours later his plane touched down in Des Moines. He marveled at the miles and miles of dark green corn fields and realized how much he had missed that color. When he stepped out of the terminal and was hit by the Iowa humidity, he decided maybe the mountains were just as good.

Sandy drove to their office where Cutter loaded the remaining boxes and both said their goodbyes to their office mates. They returned home where Cutter was amazed to find Sandy had apparently gone through a severe bout of a de-nesting urge, and almost everything was packed up and ready to move. She had made the executive decision they would move the day after she came home from the hospital and not wait until the school year was to begin. Cutter silently tried to figure out how he could get someone to go to their house in

Columbus to clean up the pizza boxes and bathroom gradeaux. Over the next two days, they finished packing and the moving company picked it all up. The family moved into a hotel.

And then they waited. Cutter took Jordan around to see her friends and have some final Des Moines adventures. In that it was still Des Moines, those adventures didn't take all that much time. Sandy did not take to the waiting game too well, so after two days, she went on line to find out how she might move the process along more quickly. She found two suggestions: vigorous exercise or vigorous sex. The exercise didn't seem to work. Happily, the sex did, though it was difficult with Jordan asleep in the same room. Thirty minutes after Cutter had finished his connubial duties and was snoring away, Sandy felt the first pang. She decided she would let Cutter get some sleep before waking him to keep her company. After the second pang, she said "Fuck it," and woke him up.

Cutter wanted to leave for the hospital immediately. He had heard the stories of how the second child comes lots sooner, and he wanted to avoid delivering Junior in an elevator or the back seat of the car. Sandy insisted they wait and at six in the morning, they carried Jordan to the car, dropped her at a friend's house and were at the hospital by seven. They spent eight more hours playing Lamaze. A game both silently decided they didn't like. They finally got to the big finale.

When the doctor said it was time and Junior was crowning, Cutter moved from Sandy's side to witness

76

the birth of their son. Early in the pregnancy Cutter had asked her doctor what it felt like to give birth. She told him to take each end of his upper lip between his thumbs and forefingers. Once Cutter had hold of his lip, the doctor said, "Okay. Now pull your lip over the back of your head." One look at the top of the baby's head and Cutter understood the doctor had not been kidding. It was more than enough to convince Cutter to move back to Sandy's side.

With the final herculean push, she dug her fingernails into Cutter's palm so hard she drew blood. The sound of sloshing liquid and Junior was out and yelling. The doctor handed him to Cutter who held his son gently in the palm of the hand that was bleeding. There Sandy's blood mingled with Cutter's. If anyone had asked him at that instant how it felt, Cutter would have told them it was as if someone had bestowed upon him a great, maybe THE great, truth--understanding that if he were to actually say it, it would somehow diminish the purity of the truth. He had worried that having a second child might lessen the love he felt for Jordan. What he found was his capacity to love was doubled, instantly. Christ in a handbasket, this was amazing.

The next few days were a blur. Introducing Jordan to her new brother, naming Junior (they settled on Livingston, though Cutter claimed to prefer Fred, after his pet chicken), enduring the visits from the grandparents, enduring the hate-to-see-you-leave's from friends, making a final check that all Iowa business was indeed done, and packing up Sandy's SUV for the 15 hour drive to their new home.

In fact, the next three months were pretty much a blur. Neither Cutter nor Sandy had realized two kids took more effort than one times two. It was more like one times six. You never got a break. Before, they could relieve each other taking care of Jordan. Now it was work, kids, work, kids, work, kids, sleep, interrupted by kids. Oh, and all exacerbated by Jordan's newest acquisition, a small, white, furry, yappy dog which she named, as promised, Baily. When the baby stopped crying and Jordan quit talking or whining, the dog was there to take up the slack by chiming in with its shrill little bark. As Cutter had anticipated, it took about four weeks for the excitement of having a pet to wear off. He found himself responsible for walking the damn thing and cleaning up its accidents. He soon learned to hate the foul little mutt.

But then, there were times in those months Cutter and Sandy hated each other. Blamed each other for the continuous state of exhaustion and irritability. They snapped at each other. They pouted. They whined. Their sex life went from sixty to zero. Okay, maybe forty-five to zero, but still. As a weak protest to prove he wasn't losing his manhood completely, Cutter decided to grow a beard. He had never had facial hair before and discovered he really liked not having to shave. Even though everyone agreed his red scraggly, patchy beard was one of the ugliest anyone had ever seen, he refused to remove it. When he looked in the mirror, he saw Ernest Hemingway.

Their work lives didn't help that much. Sandy felt as if she had to give more than 100% in that she had gotten a late start on helping at the Parks and Recreation Department. Cutter finally began to feel the effects of a job that required not just fifty hours at work each week, but in truth was with him all of his waking hours and some of his few sleeping ones. Once his staff had gotten through the initial want-to-curry-favor-with-the-new-guy phase, they threw themselves whole-heartedly into Phase Two: let's test the limits of this guy. This second phase was intensified by Sandy's presence. The staff had been told she was there to help with finances and planning, but it didn't take long for folks to see Cutter seemed to always bend to her directions. And it didn't take long for them to start resenting her. Fortunately for Cutter, both Alicia and Rachel had already decided that their loyalty lay with him. Partly because, as Alicia put it, "If I used the 'B' word, which I don't, I'd use it for her," referring to Sandy.

Phase Two came to a head during a staff meeting in November. Cutter was setting out his budget for capital improvements which included how much he wanted to spend on new parks and facilities and on renovations to existing ones. Alan Wells, a landscape architect who was the head of planning and apparent leader of the opposition to Cutter and Sandy, chose this issue to draw his battle line. Before Cutter could get ten minutes into his presentation, Alan stood up.

"Excuse me, Director Williams, but this isn't the way we do the budget here. My staff and I decide what improvements have priority, and then we send it to Rachel who does the actual budgeting work. Then you, as director, forward it on to the city's Finance Department and to the City Council." Cutter looked around at the eight faces in front of him. Five smiles, three looks of concern—only Alicia, Rachel and Jerry Picker, head of maintenance, appeared to not welcome this confrontation. That left the assistant director of programming, the assistant director of facilities, the human resources manager, the head of public information and fund raising and the special projects manager all squarely on the side of the usurper.

"And why is it done that way?" Cutter asked in a very quiet and earnest voice.

Alan smiled. "Well, as you know, I am a registered landscape architect. As are several members of my staff. We are all professionally trained not only to plan parks but also to decide on what facilities are the best for the public. It would be hard to explain to someone who has no real experience in the field." With that, Cutter noticed that even the usurper's supporters were looking down and avoiding his eyes. Alan failed to notice he was losing his backers and continued. "You see, Cutter, this is something best left to the professionals."

Alan started to sit and Cutter patted the air upwards to have him remain standing. "Just a minute. I've been studying this parks thing a little and have a few questions." Alan continued to smile but with obvious chagrin. If Cutter wanted a fight, Alan would give it to him. Now was as good a time as any. Bob Wayne had understood

Alan was in charge of this budget and function, and it was time Cutter learned the same thing.

Cutter went on, "From what I have read, there were a handful of folks who influenced our modern day urban parks and recreation. Those guys who really led the way to what we all believe makes a city a good place to live. To name a few, Frederick Law Olmstead, designer of New York's Central Park; John Muir who first established natural areas; Teddy Roosevelt who established the national parks system; James Naismith and Abner Doubleday and Alexander Cartwright who gave us basketball and baseball respectively; Daniel Burnham who gave us the concept of interconnected urban parks; and Robert Moses who definitively demonstrated the economic value of parks to cities. You've heard of them?" Cutter noticed Alan had quit smiling. "Well?"

"Sure I've heard of them."

"Olmstead: journalist. Muir: author. Roosevelt: rancher, politician, soldier. Naismith: doctor. Doubleday: soldier. Cartwright: bookseller. Burnham: building architect. Moses: political scientist. You beginning to see a pattern here, Al? Anyone?"

Rachel smiled, "Gee, Cutter, not a landscape architect among them. What do you suppose that means?" Cutter couldn't have written her script any better.

Cutter continued, "I think we're done here for the day." Alan Wells stomped out and the others quickly filed out behind him, no one looking at anything other than the floor. Rachel was the last to the door and Cutter said to her back, "Rachel, could you stay for a couple of minutes?"

"Sure, boss. What do you need?"

"Did I just screw the pooch?"

"Uh, I don't know. I don't know what that means."

"Sorry. Did I screw it up with staff by attacking Alan?"

"I don't think so, Cutter. In fact, I think he thought maybe he was in charge. Both Theresa Blackman and Bob let him do whatever he wanted. I think he is small minded and self-serving."

"But some of the others seemed to take his side."

"Only because they are used to doing things their own way and want to continue doing so. After our last two directors, it's tough having a new sheriff in town. So to speak. They'll be fine. Anything else?"

"Yeah. Do you think my capital improvements plan is actually okay? Do we have the money to cover it?"

Rachel thought for a moment. "Yeah. We can make it work. But obviously it doesn't solve our biggest problem—Riverside Park. The infrastructure there is so old and so in need of renovations which could run to the tens of millions of dollars. Eventually it's going to catch up with us."

Cutter said, more to himself than her, "Maybe that's why that reporter asked me about Riverside." Then to Rachel, "Okay. Thanks. Let's go talk to Sandy and see if we can get her blessing." He was only half kidding.

At home that evening, after Jordan and Livingston had been fed and played with and put to bed, Cutter sat in the den, staring at but not seeing the endless list of numbers on the computer screen. He decided that the only thing he hated more than budgets was Humphrey's staff meetings. Just as his eyes began to blur over, Sandy put her hand on his shoulder.

"Buy you a drink, sailor?" and she handed him a glass with three fingers of bourbon. Well, this is a nice change of pace, he thought. Sandy sat in the overstuffed easy chair next to the desk, glass of wine in her hand. She sighed and said, "I heard about your staff meeting today. The office chatter was about how you really nailed Alan to the wall. Seems he has fewer friends on staff than we thought." She smiled. "Though I think you have an enemy now that you will need to keep an eye on."

"Mistake?"

"Nope. Exact opposite I think. And you're my hero."

Cutter grinned. Not so much at what Sandy had said, but at the fact that he could palpably feel the ice of the last several months melt. "So, wanna get laid by your hero?"

"Gee, Cutter, I wasn't sure you were ever going to get the idea…" She stood, took his hand and led him upstairs.

Afterwards they lay in bed, sipping their drinks in the dark. Cutter finally whispered, "Thanks. I think I needed that." Sandy purred. He continued, "Maybe we need to get away for a few days, just you and me. What do you think?"

"Mmmm," was her only answer as she fell asleep.

Two days later, Cutter was having lunch with Cord at the Morgan House and asked him, "So Wild Bill, got any suggestions where I could take Sandy for a three or four day adult getaway?"

"What do you have in mind?"

"I'm not sure," Cutter answered. "Sandy really likes to ski, but I'm not that much into it. Maybe someplace where she could ski the tough slopes and I could do the bunny ones. But with a nice restaurant or two, all not too expensive."

Cord smiled. "I have just the place. If you don't mind a little company. Beth and I have use of the Carroll's cabin up at Slippery Slopes Ski Resort about an hour north of here. We could get the families together for a long weekend."

"I was kind of hoping to get away from the kids for a couple of days."

"Not a problem. We take the nanny to watch the kids. C'mon. It'll be fun—get the wives and kids together. Beth and I both want to meet Sandy. I think you said your daughter is the same age as ours. If we decide we don't get along, the place is big enough for everyone to escape."

"Sounds pretty expensive."

Cord twirled the end of his moustache. "Not for us, it ain't. Ty writes it all off as a business expense."

"Okay. We're in. When do you want to go?"

Instead of answering, Cord pointed across the room with his fork. "Isn't that your planning guy coming in with a couple of your commissioners?"

Cutter turned and watched Alan walk in, deep in conversation with Steve Barker and Wade Taylor, both members of the parks commission. Steve was a professor at Central Western State where he taught Native American history and culture. Steve was the commission's resident expert in wilderness recreation. Wade was a local developer and often served as the commission's representative in land acquisition negotiations. Cutter liked them both. He mentally ran through the list of upcoming projects, trying to recall if they were working on an acquisition of a wilderness area. He couldn't remember anything that might involve both Steve and Wade. Made a mental note of the meeting and turned his attention back to Cord.

"So when can we go skiing?"

"How about weekend after next?"

"Sounds good."

As Cutter and Cord finished lunch and left, carefully avoiding Alan and the commissioners, Alan was making his case to Steve and Wade. "I asked you to lunch because I wanted to give you both a heads up on what I believe is a very serious problem." Alan had worked many times with both men and considered them friends.

Professor Barker raised his bushy white eyebrows and asked, "What problem is that?"

"Well, frankly, I don't like to talk out of class, but I sincerely think Director Williams is going to ruin the department. I know it's not my place to criticize the boss, but you guys are both friends and I wanted to warn you before it is too late."

Wade wanted to know, "How is he going to ruin the department?"

Alan smiled inwardly, "He knows nothing about park planning or acquisition. He refuses to take the advice of the professionals on the staff. He seems to let his wife, who isn't an employee, make all the important decisions. We don't even know why she's there. He spends a lot of time with politicians and out in the field talking with the workers. Then he uses whatever complaints those employees may have and orders their bosses to make changes, without considering what the supervisors have to say. The maintenance guys and recreation folks like him, but only because he is letting them do things the way they want. The professional staff is getting very discouraged."

Wade said, "I see. Have you talked to anyone else about your concerns?"

"In fact, I have. This morning I met with the mayor to let him know what was going on. And I'm willing to go talk with council members if you guys would like me to."

Steve slowly nodded his head and asked, "What did Mayor Humphrey say?"

"Oh, he is quite concerned. He told me that he is going to look into the situation right away and talk to Mr. Stalter about it. He thanked me profusely for coming in and said he would get back to me very soon."

Both Steve and Wade nodded in agreement and assured Alan they too would look into the situation.

By the beginning of the following week, no one was taking or returning Alan's calls. By mid-week, it finally dawned on him his coup attempt had failed miserably. Thursday night he stopped at a bar on the way home and had more than enough drinks to erase his anger and disappointment. Which was also enough to get him arrested for a DUI after he left the bar. He spent the night in jail.

Friday morning he didn't go to work. His wife Ann called Cutter to tell him what happened and to plead with Cutter not to fire Alan. Cutter assured her he understood and would take absolutely no action. He even asked her if there was anything he could do to help. Ann cried and said, "No. But thank you so much. We will always be indebted to you."

Cutter hung up, leaned back and put his feet up on the desk. A huge grin spread across his face. Keep your friends close. Keep your enemies closer.

EIGHT

Sandy was more than a little excited to hear about the ski trip plan. Especially the part about the nanny. She called Beth to introduce herself and invited her to lunch. After she made sure Beth was okay with the idea, and it wasn't some wild, hare-brained scheme Cutter had cooked up with his golfing buddy. They decided on Saturday, so Jordan could come along and meet Beth and Cord's daughter Sabrina. Downtown, where afterwards maybe they could even do a little shopping for ski clothes.

Sandy and Jordan arrived at La Maison des Vingt-Sept Femmes first and told the hostess the reservation was in the name of Beth Richards. Even though this was the beginning of the busy ski season and there were people waiting, they were immediately whisked to a corner table overlooking the quaint street filled with beautiful people buying beautiful skiwear. No sooner had they sat down, than the owner/chef, Bradford Q, was greeting them and taking their drink order. Jordan had just taken a sip from her Shirley Temple when she suddenly squealed loudly and jumped up yelling, "Sabri, Sabri," at a little girl who had just walked in.

"Mommy, that's Sabri, my newest and bestest friend," she told Sandy. Jordan was beside herself when it turned out that Sabrina and her mom were their lunch dates. Beth and Sandy introduced themselves and were laughing about Columbus being a small town indeed when Bradford Q suddenly appeared at the table with a glass of wine for Beth and a hot chocolate for Sabrina.

"*Mme Richards, c'est tellement agréable de vous joindre à nous à nouveau.*"

"*Merci,*" Beth responded, without a trace of self-consciousness. And with a perfect accent, "*C'est agréable de vous revoir.*"

Before Sandy could ask about the French or the owner or the special treatment they were getting, Jordan was tugging on her arm and handing her the Shirley Temple. "Mom, I don't like this! Can I have a hot chocolate too? Please, Mom, please. Just like Sabri has."

"Yes, dear. I'll order it when the waiter comes to see what we want. What would you like to eat?" Sandy asked her. "How about a nice salad?"

Jordan made her yuck face and replied, "Oh, Mom, Sabri and I don't like salad. We want noodles with butter and nothing else."

"Sorry, kiddo, they don't have that on the menu."

"But that's what we want. Don't we, Sabri?"

Sandy, her face beginning to redden, looked at Beth, who crinkled her forehead and smiled. "Sorry. Sabrina is a little picky. That's our word for 'spoiled'." With that, Beth raised her left index finger just above her shoulder, a subtle gesture to summon the invisible waiter behind her. He appeared in three seconds, as if by magic. Beth asked Sandy, "What would you like to eat?"

"The Nicoise Salad, please."

Beth turned to the waiter, "Could you please bring Jordan a hot chocolate? My friend would like the *salade niçoise,* and I'll have the *joues de porc braise.* And would you be so kind to ask BQ if he'll fix some pasta with butter for the girls?"

"Certainly, Ma'am," the waiter said and then disappeared, again as if by magic.

Sandy, who was not used to being impressed, was impressed. "For a girl from Colorado, you sure seem to know your way around a French restaurant."

Beth laughed gently. "Probably even more surprising for a girl from Baltimore. And not the big Baltimore. I'm from the one in Ohio. And from the wrong side of the tracks there. I was raised on the Basil side of town. Out by the lumber yard, where my daddy worked. But I have had a very lucky life."

"How so?" Sandy asked.

"After college—where I did take a couple of years of French, just in case I ever got the chance to go to France—I got my first job as an assistant to the publisher of a small group of suburban newspapers outside of Cincinnati, Ohio. That's where I met Cord, and, well, we…" Beth's voice trailed off and she blushed slightly.

Sandy picked right up on it. "Sounds like a story."

Beth leaned in, whispering, "You've heard of being swept off your feet? It was kind of the sexual equivalent of that. We were on a negotiating team together and celebrated after the negotiations finished and ended up in bed together. Luckily, it turned out he was great husband material."

Sandy smiled. "Lord, it's been a long time since I've had any girl talk. This is great. So I have to ask. Was he that good?" She giggled.

Now Beth giggled. "Good enough I just had to marry him. That night I actually passed out from the orgasm. No way I was going to let this one get away." Beth paused. "I can't believe I told you that." She blushed. "How did you and Cutter meet?"

"We worked together. Off and on for five years. Then he finally asked me out and I thought he was just joking." Sandy went on to share her story with Beth while they finished lunch, which included a chocolate tart for each of the girls. They decided to shop for a while, as it turned out, a three hour adventure where both Sandy and Jordan got three new ski outfits each. The shopping barely got in the way of the conversation.

"Tell me about the excellent French."

"Oh, it's just passable. Here in Colorado I don't get much chance to use it. One of the reasons we go to Bradford's place. He humors me by only speaking French to me."

Sandy kept digging. "How did you learn to speak it so well?"

"Cord and I spent six months in Paris, right before we moved out here. It was something I had always wanted to do, and when Mr. Carroll offered Cord the job, Cord was thoughtful enough to make six months off part of the deal." Anyway, we lived in a very small 400 square foot apartment on Avenue de Lowendal. Spent the first three weeks doing all the tourist things, museums, churches, art galleries, bookstores, fountains, and chateaus. What I learned quickly is my college French didn't get me very far. Whenever we went into a store or restaurant, I would prepare what I was going to say and would say it perfectly. Sadly, they would answer in French and I would rarely understand a word of it. So I would just stand there, gaping and looking lost. Cord called it my deer in the headlights look." She smiled at the memory.

"So I took classes while we were there. And spent the next five months learning the real Paris, off the beaten track, where not everyone spoke English. Tourist Paris is wonderful, but real Paris is so much better.

"Anyway, many nights we ate at the restaurant right outside the front door of our apartment building, a place named Le Sept Quinze. When we finally moved here, we found Bradford's place and since it also had Sept in the name, we took it as a sign it should be our restaurant."

"Does '*sept*' have some special meaning? Is it some kind of culinary term?"

"Lord, no. It means 'seven'. Just the number. Le Sept Quinze means 715. Bradford's place, when translated means 'House of the 27 Women'. He claims that is the number of women he has slept with. No one believes him." Beth laughed loudly. "But we humor him anyway. Cord does almost all his business dinners and lunches there. We're probably BQ's biggest customers."

Sandy laughed as well. They talked about their kids and their husbands. In addition to Sabrina, Beth and Cord had a two year old daughter named Theano. Sandy asked about the choice of names. "I picked Sabrina. I hate to admit it, but I got it from an old movie. Cord picked Theano. He said he read it someplace, but I later found out it was the name of a girl he dated in college. I don't think he ever got over her completely. When I asked him about it, he just got pissed. I leave it alone now, but I started calling her Teá."

They talked about places to shop and places to eat. About Sandy's work and about Beth's volunteering for a child advocacy group. About their families back in Iowa and Ohio. By the end of the day, Sandy decided that it was going to be like going on a ski vacation with old friends. She was as excited about the friends part as she was about the ski part.

Cutter spent the day with Livingston, which mostly consisted of letting him sleep, changing his diaper, letting the damn dog out hourly and pretending to work on budgets while really watching the Northwestern Wildcats basketball team get their asses handed to them by Loyola. Being a Wildcats fan was almost as disheartening as being a Cubs fan. And don't even mention da Bears. Maybe it was time to switch to the Broncos.

"Daddy! Daddy! Look at what I got. New ski clothes! And we're going skiing with my best friend, Sabri. Can you believe it? It's so exciting. I can't wait 'til next week." With that, Jordan flew up the stairs to try on her new clothes.

Cutter looked up at his wife's smiling face. "I take it your day went well? Jordan likes Cord's daughter? And you? You like Beth?"

"Turns out Jordan and Sabrina were already friends at school. And, yeah, I like Beth. She's funny and fun. And, Daddy, I got some new ski clothes as well." She held up a new ski jacket and whirled around. "I even got you a jacket so you won't be tempted to wear that glow-in-the-dark green parka." She tossed him a stylish jacket and followed Jordan up the stairs. Cutter looked at the price tag and whistled. Glad he wasn't in charge of the family finances.

The next day, he called Cord to confirm the trip and to get directions. Cord told him, "We'll pick you guys up. Actually, we'll be taking the company van up. They'll pick us up and drop us off at the cabin. Beth and I have already had the kitchen and bar stocked—our treat. We'll see you about five Friday evening. Be back by the kids' bedtime on Monday. Sound okay?"

It sounded perfect to Cutter.

The ride up to Slippery Slopes was from the front of a Hallmark Christmas card. It had snowed earlier in the day, but the night was like crystal and the roads almost as clear. The stars were miniature fireworks. The girls drank hot chocolate from thermoses and the adults shared a bottle of wine. Cutter was surprised to see the resort was the reverse of any he had been to. At Slippery Slopes, the lodges, condos, cabins, restaurants and shops were on top of the mountain, so you skied down from the lodge and the lifts took you back home. Of course, the only ski resorts Cutter had ever been to were a couple of trips to Snowstar in Andalusia near the Quad Cities and one trip up to Alpine Valley outside of Madison. Both of those "resorts" would have fit on one quarter of one of Slippery Slopes' mountains. If they were combined. Cutter thought maybe he had bitten off more than he could chew.

Cutter was not sure what he expected, but the Carroll ski cabin was not unlike many of their holdings, modest only in name. It had a great room; catering kitchen; library (with pool table); six bedrooms, all suites with their own bars and refrigerators; a total of ten baths, including one that featured an eight person Jacuzzi, a steam bath and a sauna; and an indoor lap pool, all contained in 14,000 square feet of heavily varnished wood with ceilings that rose to 35 feet in the main areas. And square in the center of the great room was a 35 foot Colorado Blue Spruce Christmas tree decorated with thousands of lights and hundreds of gleaming bulbs. When the girls saw it, they squealed with delight. Cutter had to restrain himself from doing the same thing.

They made themselves a light dinner, turned the children over to the nanny and explored the house with their after dinner drinks. It did not escape Cutter's notice that Sandy had stars in her eyes, but then so did he. They finally alit in the library, where they played eight ball—men against the women—and began to get to know each other as couples. Both couples had couples friends, but in all those cases, it was girl friends who dragged along their husbands, or visa-versa. This seemed different to all four of them. They all seemed to get along, in any combination of two, three or four. The women won three games easily. Turned out that Sandy had wasted more than a few hours hanging out with her older brothers at the local pool hall.

By ten o'clock they trundled off to their suites, excited for the skiing the next day. Except for Cutter, who was realizing that he was not ready for this kind of skiing.

There are four kinds of skiers: beginners, slow skiers, competent skiers and skiers who attack the mountain as if it were an unruly subject to be beaten into submission. Cutter would have liked to think he was just a slow skier, but here, he would have to catch up to qualify as a beginner. Both Beth and Sandy were competent and Cord was clearly an attacker.

After they got Jordan and Sabrina safely ensconced in ski school/camp and the nanny received her instructions on the proper care of Theano and Livingston and of when to pick up the girls, the adults took to the slopes. Cord went in search of black diamonds, the women skied together on some of the longer runs and Cutter, thankful not to have to show off his incompetence in front of the others, made his way to the baby bunny slope. Though three degrees hardly counted as a slope. After a couple of hours, he felt comfortable enough to try an actual downhill run, and he made it to the bottom safely, if not quickly. In fact, except for the three falls and the ride back up in a 75 foot high open-air chair lift designed to test the limits of his acrophobia, he kind of enjoyed the experience. Decided he might fit in. Even in his glow-in-the-dark green parka.

They met for lunch and to check in on the girls and then returned to their respective slopes, after agreeing to meet at four o'clock for one final run together and, yes, they would do it at Cutter's pace. Cutter spent the next two hours trying to feel comfortable enough that he wouldn't embarrass himself in front of the others. At least they had agreed to take the longest green circle run for his benefit.

At the appointed hour, they met and started down the hill. It soon became apparent to all that no one could possibly go as slow as Cutter did, so he released them and told them he would meet them at the bar in the lodge. He puttered his way down the hill and caught the ski lift back up the mountainside, truly happy that the day's adventure was coming to a close. He was tired. He was wet. And he was getting cold.

Cutter had been raised Catholic and practiced the religion, off and on, into his mid-twenties. Somewhere along the way he developed questions about his faith. And not just the Catholic faith but any faith. It seemed to him that the idea of existing for eternity was a truly discomforting thought. How could any sentient creature who could comprehend the concept of endless time not realize that a mind could not withstand the pressure of endlessness? Eventually the consciousness would have to go mad or at least change so much that the essence that entered eternity would not be recognizable, even to

97

itself. And if that were true, why would there need to be a construct like heaven and hell, and if there were no need for those things, why would there need to be the concept of a god, except maybe for those people who need an explanation for the random tics of fate. It wasn't so much that Cutter sought to find answers to these questions. It was more that he thought maybe if he just hung around long enough, the answers would find him. So he spent little time thinking about post death. When Sandy had asked him whether they should get Livingston baptized, he told her, "You know I don't really believe in that stuff, but I've been wrong about lots of things. I don't think we should risk Livingston's afterlife on my beliefs." Sandy had just smiled and arranged for the baptism.

Halfway up the mountain, the chair lift stopped abruptly, leaving Cutter dangling about in the wind, 75 feet above the rocky ground below. And when something in the cable snapped and he plunged 15 feet and barely managed to stay in the chair, he revisited his whole perspective of God. In fact, he had a nice conversation with the old fellow that went something like, "God, if you let me get off this chair alive, I promise I will never, ever get back on a ski lift again." He had pretty much that same one-sided conversation, in one form or another, over and over again during the next 45 minutes. Which was how long it took for them to get the rescue rope set up to bring him down. Cold, wet, achy.

The others went looking for him when he failed to show at the bar and, drinks in hand, they enjoyed the spectacle of his rescue. He let them buy him a drink and recounted his adventure, leaving out the part where he wet himself. He did, however, share the part about his deal with God and told them he would spend his remaining days there in the lodge bar, enjoying the fire and the abundant supply of snow bunnies. None of them felt the need to dissuade him.

The next day, the women again skied the intermediate slopes, though they did find a couple that were a little more challenging, and Cord returned to his assault on Slippery Slopes. Cutter found a great spot next to a huge fireplace where he could put up his feet, which had finally thawed out, and where he could both see the skiers and signal the barmaid when it was time for a refill. He was reading William Goldman's *The Princess Bride* for the umpteenth time and finishing his second rum toddy when Sandy came in, followed by Beth, who was on crutches and dragging a bandaged ankle. On the third run of the day, she and Sandy had crossed skis and she had fallen awkwardly. The house doctor, Charlie Dwan, retired from real doctoring and doing this just for the toddies and bunnies, had ruled the injury a deep sprain and told Beth to say off it for a week. Two down. Two to go. Cutter was happy to have the company.

Cord agreed to escort Sandy if she was willing to try a few black diamond runs with him. They finished out the last half of the trip exactly like that. Cutter and Beth by the fireplace; Sandy and Cord attacking the mountain. The four of them and the kids relaxing when the skiing was over. On the drive home, Beth turned to Sandy and said, "You guys just have to come to our New Year's Eve party. It's our one big party of the year. You'll love it. And it's formal, so we get to wear our best. Fun."

"Oh, thank you. We'd love to. I was thinking Cutter needed a tuxedo anyway. That's what I'll get him for Christmas."

Damn. He'd had his eye on the newest TaylorMade driver and had hoped that would be his present. Christ in a handbasket.

NINE

A couple of weeks later, Sandy and Cutter packed up the kids and flew to Iowa for Christmas. Cutter hadn't been able to decide how to handle requests for leave for all the employees who wanted Christmas Eve off. Seems that other directors before him had done everything from deny all leaves to run a lottery to see who would get time off. In staff meeting, he asked Alicia what she thought. "Honestly, Director, I don't even know why we work that day at all. Nothing gets done. Everybody who does work tries to sneak out early."

Cutter thought for a moment. "So maybe we just give everybody the day off. Hell, just make it an official holiday."

Alicia asked, "Can we do that?"

Cutter raised his eyebrows in the form of a question to Rachel. "You're in charge, Cutter. You can probably do anything you want. Besides, who'd complain?"

Cutter smiled and told them, "Okay. Here's the deal. We need one person to man the phones here in case we get any emergencies. Supervisory staff has to understand they are on call. Each of you is to tell your staff that YOU arranged for them to get Christmas Eve off as an extra holiday." He looked at his hands. "Who's gonna cover the phones?" When he heard the voice that said "I will," his head snapped up. It was Alan. Well Merry Fucking Christmas. Another Christmas miracle.

As his now happy staff hustled out of the room, he called at Alan's back, "Thanks for taking the bullet. I owe you one." Alan only smiled in response.

Iowa Christmas was as hectic as always. Back and forth between families, working in a few friends, lots of eating, even more drinking and the kids being overwhelmed by the cornucopia of gifts. It was great to see his parents and brothers and sisters, all of whom were invited to come to the mountains for winter vacation (though Cutter knew that most, if not all, would pass on the invitations). As promised (or from Cutter's perspective, threatened), Sandy got him a tuxedo. The closest thing he got to his desired golf club was the requisite gigantic bag of tees in his stocking. To go with the dozen bags of tees he already had in the garage.

They were both relieved to be back in Columbus, especially Sandy who had seemed edgy the entire trip back home. She spent the three days after Christmas shopping for a formal gown for New Year's Eve. Cutter had never seen her quite as excited as she was about this party. She finally settled on a black floor length gown that was startlingly simple. It was low cut and very tight and left nothing to the imagination, except that it somehow managed to leave everything to the imagination. For the second time in a month, Cutter whistled at one of her clothing purchases. This time, however, it had nothing to do with the price.

On the last evening of the year, after the kids had been packed off to the sitter's, Cutter and Sandy shared a split of champagne as they dressed for the Richards' party. They had decided it had been the most momentous year of their life together, even more than the year of their fishing adventure at the Outer Banks, and that it needed to be sent out in style. Sandy seemed especially touched when he presented her with two champagne flutes that were inscribed with "A Year to Remember." Cutter thought he saw a tear in her eye. He patted himself on the back. He scored even more points when he shaved off his scraggly beard.

As Cutter finished dressing, he stood in front of the mirror, admiring the way he looked in the tuxedo. He gently pinched the corners of his bow tie between his forefingers and thumbs and gave it an imperceptible adjustment. He raised the corner of his lip in a slight sneer and said, "Bond. James Bond." Decided he may have to replace his old fantasy with a new one where he was a super spy. "Oh, I could tell you. But then I'd have to kill you." Actually he had three other fantasies. The first involved waving to the crowd from the Swilcan Bridge at St. Andrew's after winning the British Open. The second was staring at the words "The End" on his computer as he sat back with the realization he had just written THE Great American Novel. Those two fantasies he'd keep. The one he would replace is where he looked into the mirror, cowled his eyelids and said, very quietly, "I'm......Batman."

They arrived at the Richards' house fashionably late. Actually fashionably plus another 30 minutes, which made them about the last folks to arrive. Beth greeted them at the door, and when Sandy removed her coat, Cutter noticed, with not a small amount of male ego, there was a noticeable lull in the conversation as lots of heads turned their way. Cord appeared from nowhere, chucked Cutter on the shoulder, kissed Sandy on the cheek and quickly spirited her away. Cutter watched as Cord guided her into the crowded living room, his arm around her waist. Cutter stood there, arms full of their coats and marveled at her fantastic ass.

One of the help took the coats, and Beth pointed Cutter the way to the bar. He wandered through the room, looking at all the beautiful women in expensive gowns and jewelry and the slew of tuxedoed gents who appeared to be just another adornment for these women. He ordered a drink, keeping in character, "A Vesper's martini. Gordon's gin. Shaken. Not stirred." The bartender smiled. He'd heard it before and knew his role.

"Very well, Mr. Bond. With a twist, I assume."

"Certainly," Cutter replied and turned his back to the bartender and leaned back, ankles crossed, elbows on the bar as his drink was prepared. He noticed in the corner of the room there was a large group of revelers being entertained by a man playing a baby grand piano. Cutter quickly changed characters when the bartender tapped him on the shoulder. He picked up the glass, tilted his head in a salute and said, with a very slight lisp, "So, Sascha, if he plays it for her, will he play it for me?"

Sascha didn't miss a beat. "No, Mr. Rick, Sam will only play it for her."

Cutter wandered over toward the crowd. The piano player was working his way through a rendition of *This Is All I Ask*. He was as striking as any guy Cutter could remember seeing. Longish silver hair over sharp features. Coal black eyes deep set under heavy silver eyebrows. Very trim and enough color to show the guy spent time out in the weather. Wore his tuxedo like Cutter wore jeans and a tee shirt, like it was the most comfortable thing he could find to put on. A slight smile of pleasure which showed sparkling white teeth. Cutter looked at the people looking at this guy and decided he no longer wanted to be James Bond. He wanted to be this guy.

When the song ended, Cord suddenly appeared next to the guy, with his arm still around Sandy's waist. Cord spied Cutter and waved him over. "Hey, Cutter, somebody I want you to meet." Cutter started to make his way through the throng and was a little surprised when the crowd parted for his passing.

"Cutter. Sandy. This is Ty Carroll, my boss. And our piano player for the evening."

Ty rose and offered his hand to Cutter. "Pleased to meet you, young man. I've heard a lot of good things about you." He turned to Sandy, took her hand, kissed it and said, "And Mrs. Williams, I see you are not just the brains of the operation. You got all the looks as well. I trust my friend Mr. Richards is taking good care of you."

"Oh, you bet," Cutter replied. "Very good care. In fact, we want to thank you so much for letting us stay at your ski cabin with them. That was very generous of you."

"Think nothing of it. Glad to see it's getting some use. My kids are grown and the wife doesn't like skiing that much, so we're happy to see it used. Feel free to stay anytime you want. You don't even have to take Cord and Beth with you."

Sandy was all smiles. "Thank you. We may take you up on that offer, though we'd have to take the Richards along since Cutter has sworn off skiing."

"Well, I understand from President Eggleston you two are doing a bang up job with the parks. Glad to hear that. The operation seemed to be in a mess and going downhill quickly. Makes a big difference to our community. Keep up the good work and do let me know if there is any way I can help you." He flashed his bright smile at them. "Better get back to the music. Don't want to lose my audience. They're hard to come by as it is." He winked at Cutter and sat back down at the piano, where he riffed off a handful of notes to announce his return.

Beth showed up and claimed Sandy, and Cord took Cutter on the rounds to meet the other guests. Some he knew, though he did note that not one elected official was there. He had assumed he would at least see Ham and Eggs. He did run into one of his commission members, Steve Barker, and was amused to see that it was still two hours until the New Year arrived, and Steve was already slurring his words. Cutter guessed the first time Steve would see the New Year would be sometime tomorrow. Which turned out to be the case. The evening passed pleasantly and at midnight, when the ball dropped, Cutter and Sandy were dancing, Cutter with both of his left feet. They held their kiss for a long time and promised each other the New Year would be the best yet.

It didn't start out too great. In mid-January, Livingston developed pneumonia and had to be hospitalized. Both parents had several sleepless days and nights, but he recovered nicely and was up and about by the end of the month. February didn't go much better. The budgets for the city passed, and once again, Parks and Recreation's operating budget took a hit. Cutter wasn't going to have to lay anyone off, but he would not be able to fill vacancies over the next six to eight months. The staff grew more disheartened. By March, everyone was ready for winter to be over (save ski resort owners), and cabin fever had set in. The only thing that kept Sandy and Cutter from killing each other was the fact that Sandy chose to spend more and more time out of the office, if for no other reason than to give them a little separate time. When anyone, including Cutter, asked what she was doing she told them she was trying to develop new funding sources for the department.

April and the winter finally broke. Cutter marked his first year on the job, pleased he and Sandy had managed to keep the department together, disappointed they didn't seem to be making any progress towards improving it. Sandy lifted his spirits in the middle of the month by telling him, "I think Rachel and I have identified a potential way of having our own tax revenue. I'm going to go up to Denver next week and meet with some folks to find out if it can and should be attempted."

He told her, "Great. Let's have lunch and you can tell me all about it."

"I can't. I have another meeting. We'll talk tonight."

That afternoon, a group of maintenance employees came to see Cutter to warn him that the equipment they were being asked to use was so old and in such bad shape they were putting him on official notice. If one of the employees was injured using worn equipment, as director he would be held accountable and they would sue him. He assured them he would try to help. He spent the rest of the afternoon with Rachel trying to figure out how to come up with the money.

All in all, it was a helluva crappy day. All Cutter wanted to do was go home, have a beer and leave it behind. When he arrived, he entered as quietly as he could, not because anyone might be asleep, but because at home Sandy had been on a tear the last couple of days, touchy and grumpy, and he knew enough to walk on eggshells when she was in that mood. He assumed it was PMS related, though in fact he had no idea when that occurred, or even if it did. As he walked through the house he met Sandy coming out of the kitchen, drying her hands on the tail of her shirt. He held out his arms to offer a hug. She furrowed her brow, slitted her eyes and barked, "What?"

"How about a hug?"

"I don't feel like hugging you right now."

"Why not?"

"Because you owe me an apology."

"Okay. I'm sorry. What did I do?"

"You know exactly what you did. And if you don't, it's even worse."

Cutter stood there, arms spread, panic surging through him. A deer in a sharpshooter's scope had more of a chance. He ran through the possibilities: forgot to do something, said something in the wrong tone of voice, yelled at Jordan or Livingston, left the toilet seat up, farted in company, kicked the damn dog. By the time he ticked off his potential sins, it was too late. Sandy had stomped upstairs. Too late for mollification. Christ in a handbasket.

The rest of the evening was no better. Nor the rest of the week. Cutter and Sandy did not speak, except about and through the children, before she left for Denver. The following Monday morning, she drove herself to the airport after leaving him a note which said she would be back Thursday and would try to call the kids that night. When she called the first night, Jordan answered the phone, chatted for a few minutes and hung up before Cutter could talk to her. Cutter knew eventually she would get over whatever it was, but still, it pissed him off. She phoned two days later and seemed in a much better mood, almost chatty, and told him about her meeting with the Parks and Recreation Association folks and their state senator. Cutter was surprised to hear about the second meeting and wondered how Sandy had gotten in to see her so easily. She told Cutter she would be home the following evening.

That same week, Ty Carroll and Cord Richards attended a Colorado Media Executives Association meeting also in Denver. For the most part, it was less meeting and more hobnobbing, but it gave the print and electronic media moguls a chance to get away from their spouses and commiserate with their colleagues. In fact, Ty and Cord saw little of each other all week. One of the few times they did, they were with a group of newspaper publishers which was trying to close down a bar on Monday night.

"I tell you, Ty, this is going to be bad for the community and a real black eye for Vail's reputation," said Tom Hicks, publisher of the *Vail Picayune*. "All the media, all the elected officials, all the resort operators and most of the business owners are for it, but this one jackass, this rabble-rouser name of Paul Timothy, has gotten the public all riled up, and now there's a special election on the issue in June. It's gonna be a fucking free for all," Hicks practically spitting out the words.

The "it" he referred to was the Jacob Matthew Cup. More commonly referred to as the Jake. Twenty years before, a group in Denver had issued a challenge to Europe to compete against North America in a winter sports competition much like the Ryder Cup in golf. The event was named after arguably the greatest skier to ever come out of Denver. Originally it was set up as a fundraiser for local charities and attracted enough participation and interest that six years later the broadcast rights were sold to a national sports channel, and it became an overnight hit. The Jake featured about four dozen individual sports from speed skating to downhill skiing but no team sports. There were no individual medals only team points. Europe had won the last three times, two years before by the biggest margin ever recorded in the event. That competition was held in Vermont.

The next Jacob Matthew Cup was slated for France next winter and the one two years after that had been awarded to Vail. For the Vail competition, all the national and international sponsors were already signed up, as were the local contributors. Construction on the arenas, housing and festival village was slated to begin in the summer. The site chosen for the new facilities was along Middle Creek on the north side of town. All was on schedule until Mr. Timothy got involved and decided the construction would ruin one of the few pristine areas left in the community. It didn't take long for the public to take up arms. Saving nature was always a big selling point to the residents of Colorado.

"So what are you guys going to do about it?" Ty asked Tom.

"Not much we can do. Sit and wait. Run some ads and editorials about all the good the event will do for the community. Hope..." his voice trailed off.

"Well, good luck. Let me know if there is any way we can help," Ty offered. He turned to Cord who had been intently listening to the conversation. Ty touched his right index finger to his temple twice quickly and blinked his eyes slowly. Cord nodded slightly to indicate, "Message received."

TEN

The following Sunday, Cutter had taken Jordan for a short trail ride at the Riverside Park stables. Sandy stayed at home with Livingston and worked on her report to the commission. She had explained to Cutter the news was not good out of Denver. There was indeed a state statute which permitted park districts to have their own tax levies, but only if they were backed by another government entity such as a school board or county government. That would mean sharing control of the department with yet another agency. And convincing the City Council to give up their pet department. Not promising. Not promising at all. Nonetheless, Sandy, at Cutter's suggestion, was preparing a report to the commission to let them make the final decision. They both knew how that would go.

"Mommy, Mommy. I got to ride a really big horse. She is black and her name is Zoey. It was sooooo fun. I'm going to get Zoey every time we go. Can Sabri go next time? Can she?" Jordan didn't wait for an answer as she flew up the stairs, Baily yapping at her heels.

"Hey, you two, try to keep quiet. I just put your brother down for a nap." Sandy was talking to empty space.

Cutter walked up behind her and hugged her. "Ew. You smell like horse," Sandy complained, but she didn't push him away. The fact was, she had been very affectionate since she returned from Denver. Apparently she just needed a few days away from them all. "Go take a shower, and then I have something to show you." He did as he was told.

Half an hour later he wandered into the office they had set up at home. "So whatcha got to show me?" Sandy entered something into the search engine and scrolled through several pages.

"This," she said. "Read this article."

He leaned over her shoulder and read the short news article.

"Vail, Colorado, April 9.

Paul Timothy, a lifelong resident of Vail, announced today his group, Citizens to Preserve Vail, has collected enough signatures on the petition for a referendum on the development along Middle Creek. The development, which had been approved by a vote of City Council, is for the facilities necessary to host the Jacob Matthew Cup in two and half years. The vote will be held in June. A representative of the local Cup committee indicated they are confident the development will be supported and the competition will go on as planned."

"So? What's the Jacob Matthew Cup? What does that have to do with us?" Cutter wondered.

Sandy explained what the event was. "Don't you see?

114

This might be the thing to get the department and our employees back in the game. If that vote stops the development of the necessary facilities, the competition will have to be moved. Why not to Columbus? It's never been here. We get out in front of this and tell the organizers we can be the backup. At least, go talk to Hugh and Eggleston. Maybe the mayor, though Humphrey doesn't have the brains God gave a goose, so he probably wouldn't see the benefit. What do you think?"

Cutter marveled at her. So typical of his wife, to spy the smallest little thing and to see the big opportunity. Just like her days in Davenport. He was so taken aback, he didn't answer.

"You think it's a stupid idea?" she asked, trying not to sound disappointed.

"Oh, no. No. I think it is fucking brilliant. Have you found any more information about it?"

Sandy closed the news article and opened a file. In it she had assembled information about the Jacob Matthew Cup, what she could find on Vail's bid to host it and a list of the facilities needed for hosting.

"What about sponsors? It looks like some big dollars will be needed."

"Good point. You read what I have here, and I'll look for that information." She emailed him the file.

An hour later, he had finished going over the file, and Sandy came into the kitchen where he had set up his laptop. "Got it," she told him. "Let's have a drink and I'll fix dinner. Then we can pick this up."

"Maybe I should call Hugh and Ham and Eggs right now to see if I can get in to see them tomorrow morning."

"Good idea."

He called and made the appointments. Three hours later dinner was finished and the kids put to bed. They got the rest of the bottle of wine and gathered at her computer. She showed him what she could find about finances and sponsorships. It appeared to them that if only the local Vail sponsors backed out, the amount needed from local government and sponsors was relatively small, though sites would have to be found for any needed facilities. Buy-in from area resorts would be an absolute must.

"Maybe you should go see Mr. Carroll as well. He did offer to help us, remember?" she told him.

"I'll talk to Hugh and Ham and Eggs first. If they like the idea, I'll see Cord and get his opinion before going to see Ty."

"Right. That makes more sense."

They were both genuinely excited. In fact, she led Cutter to the couch, listened to hear if Jordan was awake and then stripped off her clothes. It didn't take long for Cutter to get just as excited and join her. As she sat astraddle of him, she took him in her hand and whispered, "Oh, this is a much better kind of horse to ride..."

All Cutter could say was "Giddy up..."

The next morning, a smile still on his face, Cutter met Hugh Stalter for breakfast at the Morgan House. "Well, Mr. Director, what can I do for you this morning?"

"Thanks for agreeing to meet on such short notice," Cutter told him. "Let's order and then I have something to show you." The waitress brought them coffee and took their orders, a sensible bowl of oatmeal for Hugh and a less sensible order of sausage gravy and biscuits for Cutter. "Read this," Cutter said, handing him a copy of the news article from the file he had laid on the table. Hugh read it quickly.

"And?" Hugh wondered.

"Sandy and I thought maybe, if Vail rejects the development, this might be something the department could get involved in. But we want your opinion."

"Why would we want to do that? You told the commission we are having budget problems as it is. How could we afford to help with this?"

"We don't think it would take any of our money. And it might in fact bring us in some funds. We'd like to explore it with some city officials and city leaders, but only if you and the commission agree," Cutter explained.

"So far you guys haven't misled us. Let's see what some of the others think. I'll call them and get back to you. That be okay with you guys?"

"Yeah, sure, that would be great. I'm going to talk with President Eggleston a little later and feel him out, if that's okay."

"Why don't we ask him right now?" Hugh pointed to Ham and Eggs sitting across the room. They got up and walked over to Ham and Eggs' table.

"Excuse me, sir," Cutter said. "Can we interrupt you for a second?"

117

Ham and Eggs looked up and smiled. "Certainly my boy. Certainly. I can always make time for you. But aren't we meeting later? Hi, Hugh. How's it going? I trust everything's good with you. Your boy Cutter here is doing a bang-up job. Bang-up."

"Thanks, President Eggleston, we would…" Hugh said.

"Ham and Eggs, Hugh, Ham and Eggs," the council president interrupted.

They explained what Sandy and Cutter's idea was and .asked what Ham and Eggs thought.

"Crackerjack idea. Crackerjack. Go see what you can do. Also, talk to the mayor. I know, I know. He's a pain in the ass, but you don't want to blindside him. Also, you should talk to Mr. Carroll. Have you met him? I can introduce you if you like. Just let me know, boy. Glad to help."

"Will do, sir. I'll let you know how it comes out." Cutter and Hugh returned to their table and finished their breakfast. Hugh assured Cutter he would talk to the rest of the commissioners, but since he knew council would support the idea, he was pretty sure the commission would be okay with it. As long as the money side worked out.

Since he was already downtown, Cutter walked over to City Hall with the hopes of catching his honor in his office. The mayor was in but made Cutter wait thirty minutes, just on principle.

"Not much time, boy. What do you want?" Carleton Humphrey barked. Cutter explained their idea and told the mayor he had already talked with both Hugh and President Eggleston.

"Son, you don't have the time or the courtesy to participate in my cabinet, you never seem to include my office in the activities of the parks department, and you don't seem to be the least bit interested in the rest of the city government. Why the hell do you think I would want to support your plan? We're very busy. I don't have time to work on this. It's probably a pipe dream any way. I'm surprised you would even ask."

"Sorry, sir," Cutter said, biting his tongue. "I do know you're very busy. The primary reason we wanted your support is, while we would do the upfront work, the actual event would in fact require a lot of your time. The host city's official representative is expected to open and close ceremonies and spend time in the broadcast booth during the event. I should have realized you couldn't make that commitment. Sorry." Cutter stood to leave.

Carleton was flustered. "Wait. Wait a minute. Maybe since it is a long way off, I could make arrangements to participate. But there is to be no city money involved. You got that? You understand? I'll support this if you'll agree to that."

"I understand. Agreed." Cutter excused himself and left, leaving the mayor to practice his on-camera demeanor.

Cutter drove back to his office and found Sandy knee deep in papers alongside Rachel. "Rachel is helping to sort out the finances of the Jake," she told him, after he filled her in on his meetings. "The only major missing components are local sponsorships and use of the resorts. I think it's time for you to call Cord." Again, he did as told. He and Cord agreed that the best place to have this discussion, in actuality any discussion, was over beers, so they met at the Aspen Ridge Brewery. Cord arrived first and ordered both of them the 30 ounce drafts, what with it being happy hour and all.

For the fourth time that day, Cutter explained what the idea was. Probably because he was a businessman and not a politician, Cord was a lot more skeptical. "How did you come up with this idea?" he wanted to know.

"Sandy found the article about the vote. The only poll that we could find shows the vote being a dead heat right now. Thing is, no one can predict at all. Too many variables. We would like to talk to your boss about it, but I told Sandy that if you said 'no' we drop the whole thing. Are you sure you can't support it, Wild Bill?"

"I'm not saying that. We could probably get local businesses on board, both the resorts for the use of their facilities—they'll see the great free advertising it would give them—and sponsors. Transportation in and out of our airport might be a problem. It's not very big, and we have no flights to Europe. Biggest problem is where you would put new facilities. What all would have to be built?"

Cutter thought a minute and told him, "A couple of arena-style ice rinks, dormitories, a festival village, a transportation center, an exhibit hall. Luge runs at one of the resorts. Maybe some retail. Admin and maintenance buildings. I think that's about it."

"Where would you put all that stuff?"

"Not sure. Maybe Wade Taylor could help us find some land to use. Maybe some developer would like some infrastructure and building work done for him for the use of the land."

Cord continued to dig, "How long would the land have to be tied up?"

"Probably 30-32 months. No longer."

Cord thought about it a while and finished his beer. Cutter ordered them another round. "All right. Let's go talk to Ty. Tomorrow afternoon. I think he's free then. Bring Sandy along. And why don't you guys come over for dinner Saturday?"

"Great. To both. Thanks. I think this will be fun." Cutter dove into his second happy hour beer.

The next day, they met with Ty. Briefed him on their idea. Answered his few questions. Ty turned to Cord and asked, "What do you think? Should we get involved in this?"

"I'm not so sure. Seems kind of last minute. You know I think a lot of these people, and they certainly appear to know what they are doing, but we'd have a lot of catching up to do." He paused and smoothed his mustache. Then, "I think we should pass. Especially because of the land issue, not having it identified."

Ty leaned back and put his cowboy-booted feet on the desk. He smiled and winked at Cutter and Sandy, then turned to Cord. "Hell, Son, haven't I taught you anything? Any idea that's a good one has some risk. This would be great for the community. Those other things are just details. We never worry about details." He returned his attention to the Williams. "Go to Denver and talk with those people at the Jake's headquarters. I'll send Cord with you. Use our plane. We'll cover the cost of your trip, so nobody can bitch about the use of tax dollars. The sooner the better." He paused. "In fact, let's call them right now."

He jumped up and walked out to ask his secretary to get the executive director of the Jacob Matthew Cup on the line. Cutter and Sandy were smiling. Cord was not. Two minutes later Ty picked up his phone when it buzzed. "Mrs. Borin, thank you for taking my call. My name is Ty Carroll and I'm the publisher of the *Columbus City Times*." Pause. "Yes ma'am, that's me...Why, thank you. We've always been happy to help out...Yes, ma'am, there is something you could do for me. Would you be so kind as to meet with a couple of my people?...How about tomorrow afternoon? Would that be conven- ient?...Thank you so much...You bet. My assistant, Cord Richards and the couple who run our parks department, Cutter and Sandy Williams...Yes, ma'am it is a funny name...three o'clock would be perfect...Thank you so much. Bye," and he hung up.

Cutter and Sandy thanked him profusely and after making arrangements to meet Cord for the drive to the airport, left. When they were gone, Cord walked back into Ty's office and sat down. "So, boss, how do you think that went?" Ty's feet were back on the desk. "Just about perfect, I'd say. Just about fucking perfect." And he showed all his brilliant white teeth in a broad smile.

ELEVEN

Cutter had never been on a private jet before. He couldn't believe how the aircraft seemed to jump off the tarmac. This is the way to fly. No bag checks, no lines, no fees. They started the descent just as they seemed to reach cruising altitude. Sandy appeared to be really enjoying the short jaunt; Cord kept pointing out towns and landmarks to her as they flew over them. Cord was acting a whole lot more positive than he had the day before in Ty's office. Cutter thought that was a good sign.

Their meeting with Lois Borin, the executive director of the Jake, went exceptionally well. It was as if she knew why they were coming, though maybe she had heard from other suitors after the Vail news broke. At any rate, she was gracious and welcoming and encouraged them to put a proposal together to act as back up host just in case Vail had to withdraw. She assured them the national and international sponsors would stay, as would the sports channel contract. Lois suggested they get something back to her by the middle of May. The only real problem was the Jake folks wanted the location and a site plan included in the proposal.

Before they headed back to Columbus, Cord bought them an early dinner at the Buckhorn Exchange. After their drinks came, he told them, "I think the need to find a site may be a deal killer. If you guys can put together the rest of the proposal, I'll work on finding a site. Ty's family has some land, though I don't think he would want to use it for this. At worst, maybe we could tell them that's the land we would use and then pull a bait and switch."

"Okay," Cutter said. "Sandy can work out the particulars and I'll do the writing. Do you think we need to contact the resorts?"

"I think we're okay there. We might even be able to get them into a bidding war if this becomes a reality."

They finished dinner, made their way to the airport where the jet was fueled and ready to roll. Ten minutes later they were in the sky. When Cord offered, Sandy passed on a drink, but Cutter asked for an airplane gin and tonic. He had to explain to Cord what an airplane gin and tonic was. "You know, on an airplane they give you a three ounce glass filled with ice and a one and a half ounce bottle of gin, leaving room for about half an ounce of tonic." As they got their drinks, Sandy moved to the back of the plane and sat looking out the window, obviously deep in thought. Cord started to walk back to her, and Cutter grabbed his arm to stop him. "This is how she does what she does best—figuring things out." Cutter nodded toward his wife. "Best we let her ponder a while."

They chatted and fixed a second drink. Half an hour later, Sandy came up and said, "Cutter, can I see you in the back for a minute? Will you excuse us, Cord?"

"Sure. No problem."

They took facing seats at the back of the cabin and Sandy leaned in. Cutter followed suit. "Cutter, what do you think of the idea of using some existing park for this? We'd have to close it for a while, but we could get any infrastructure needs taken care of without any city money. And maybe we end up with a couple of new facilities that cost the city, and the taxpayers, nothing."

For the second time in a week, his wife's ideas left him speechless. He just stared at her.

"Well?" A little impatient.

He didn't answer. Instead, he got up and returned to the bar where Cord was sitting. "Wild Bill, let's use Riverside Park. It's the perfect size and location, it needs infrastructure renovations and we can make use of some, hell maybe all, of the new facilities for public recreation. And we control it already."

Cord looked past Cutter to Sandy, who was smiling broadly.

"Outstanding. Just outstanding. And we don't even have to tell folks it was your wife's idea." They all smiled. Sandy walked forward to them and demanded to know where her drink was. They handed her a bourbon.

She took a sip and said, "In all fairness to Cutter, I was thinking some undeveloped parkland. He came up with the Riverside idea and I think it's perfect. As much as I hate to give him credit. But as he's so fond of saying, 'Even a blind pig occasionally finds an acorn'."

Cutter grinned. "Thank you, thank you. I'll be here all week." For the benefit of his *compadres* he was making light of his idea. Internally, he was practically breaking his arm patting himself on the back. "An acorn?" She's got to be kidding. This is fucking genius, that's what it is. Make the crown jewel of the park system the center of an international event, do it for no tax dollars and get new infrastructure and facilities for the city. Acorn, my ass. This is the biggest thing since Sherlock Holmes killed Moriarty. He did kill him, right? Whatever. This is the biggest thing to hit the parks department since, well, since forever. By the time Cutter finished congratulating himself, they were landing at the Columbus airport.

On the ride back into town, Cord amended his assignments. "I'll get our attorneys working on both a draft contract and the lease for the park. Sandy, maybe you could help me put together a potential list of folks Ty should ask to be on the local committee. Cutter, you put together and then present the proposal to the parks commission and council. Seem right?"

Cutter was still being so enthralled with his brilliant idea, he didn't even notice that somehow Wild Bill had assumed control. "Yeah, I'll call Eggleston and Hugh and let them know it's coming. Shouldn't we keep this out of the news until after the Vail vote? How do we do that?"

Before Cord could respond, Sandy told Cutter "Actually, that's not a problem. State law allows both the commission and the council to hold private meetings for matters involving personnel and economic development. We'll just call this economic development."

"Great. Anything else?" Cord waited for his two companions to respond. All they did was grin. "I'll brief Ty tomorrow morning, and maybe we can meet for dinner day after tomorrow."

"Oh, why don't you and Beth come to dinner at our house? Bring the kids," Sandy suggested.

"We'll bring the wine. Hell, we'll make it champagne. Never too early to celebrate."

The following morning Cutter called Alicia, Alan, Rachel and Jerry Picker, head of maintenance, into his office. After they were seated, he closed the door and said to them, "I need for you guys to help me with a project, but before I tell you about it, you all need to agree not to discuss it with anyone. Not coworkers, not your spouses, nobody. Understood?" He looked from person to person. They were all nodding. "Do you agree?" Yes's from each one.

"What is our single biggest challenge?" he asked.

"Budget," they answered in unison.

"And why is that?"

Alan spoke up first. "Because we can't make renovations and repairs we need, because our maintenance gets further behind and because we can't try any new programs." Everyone nodded in agreement.

"Okay," Cutter said, "so let me lay out this idea and then you tell me what you think. I may have come up with a way to both let us get ahead and bring some excitement back into the department. What if I told you there is a way to eliminate one fourth of our maintenance needs for three years, build ourselves several great new facilities and do major infrastructure renovations?"

Jerry spoke first, "I don't know about the others, but I'm for it, Harry. Whatever it is." For some reason, Jerry called everyone "Harry." Cutter liked him a lot, for that and because Jerry was always willing to help in any way he could. Cutter thought maybe he should pick a name to call everyone. Since he'd given up his lifelong dream of being able to order "just a beer", maybe he could store names of beers in his memory banks instead of using that space to remember people's names. He'd have to go drinking with Jerry sometime to see if that's what he had done.

Rachel spoke, "Tell."

Cutter explained the plan to them. Of course they all knew what the Jacob Matthew Cup was, but nothing about it going to Vail or the problems there. There were a few questions, but the only one of substance was Alan's. "Why Riverside? Why not Buena Vista Park? It's closer to most of the ski resorts, it's got open land and it's in a growing neighborhood. Won't folks be upset about closing Riverside?"

"Not if we do a good enough sales job. Any other questions?"

Nobody spoke. Cutter handed out assignments, and everyone except Alan left. Then he said, "Boss, thanks for including me in this. I have to tell you, this is exciting. The best park in the city, and I get to help with its makeover. Tell me what you have in mind for this layout."

Cutter explained how he just needed a few sketches to take to the commission and council, but that they should show a village in the center of the park with a main street running parallel to the river. At the midpoint of the street Cutter wanted a village green with a performance hall on the side opposite the river. Up and down the street, buildings which would house dormitories, retail, offices and restaurants. At either end of the street big ice arenas. Support buildings that were shielded from the public eye. The arenas and performance hall situated so they could remain as permanent facilities.

They got to work. Late in the afternoon, Alan showed Cutter a rough draft, and everyone else got back to Cutter with the things he needed. Alicia made arrangements for the meetings the next afternoon with council and the commission. Somehow she had managed to get almost all of them together in one room at one time. Good girl. He was about to head out for the day when Cord called him.

"Director, Mr. Carroll would like to see you in the morning. Ten o'clock okay?" Cutter was confused by why Cord was being so stiff and formal. Before he could respond, Cord added, "Or will that interrupt your beauty sleep?" and laughed.

"You bet, Wild Bill. See you then."

"Oh, I won't be there. I'm spending the morning meeting with folks we're asking to be on the committee. It'll be just you and Ty. Don't fuck up." And he laughed again.

Cutter got to the office early the next day and was surprised to see lights on in the planning section. He wandered back there and found Alan putting the finishing touches on half dozen display boards. Alan jumped when Cutter said good morning.

"Geez, Boss, I didn't hear you come in. What time is it?"

"Seven."

"Wow. I didn't realize it was so late."

"Late? Have you been here all night?"

Alan smiled through bloodshot eyes. "Yeah, I guess I have. But I wanted to get this done," and he held up two of the boards. To Cutter they were things of beauty. Layouts, perspectives, diagrams, building facades. He had hoped for a few rough sketches. This was full out sales presentation level. His job with the commission and council just got a whole lot easier.

"Alan, I can't believe it. These are spectacular. Can't thank you enough for doing this. They're perfect. I'll just show 'em your work, and I won't have to say a thing. Thank you so much." Alan grinned. "Now go home and get some sleep."

"I'll go home and get changed. I was kinda hoping I could go with you to the meeting."

"You bet, Mr. Wells. You bet. I'm going to take them to show Mr. Carroll first, but then we'll go together to the afternoon meeting." Somehow, his enemy had become his new favorite coworker.

At a quarter to ten Cutter walked into Ty Carroll's office. Exactly two minutes later, Ty was greeting him and offering him coffee while vigorously shaking his hand. Two minutes after that, they were in Ty's office where Cutter was laying out the presentation boards. Ty looked them over and offered no comments other than things like, "Good, good" and "Yes, yes."

"Have a seat, Cutter. I have something I want to discuss with you. Before I say anything to Cord or your wife."

"Yeah?"

"I'm going to have Cord head up a committee to oversee the community's participation in the Jacob Matthew Cup. And the Carroll family will pledge one and a quarter the amount needed to cover the local contribution, though that will remain between us so we can get as many other contributors as possible. I'll also put up the guarantees. We have to make sure we have the right executive director in place. Someone we can trust and who can do the job. I want your wife to take that position. I need to know you're okay with that, having Sandy work for Cord and me."

Cutter grinned. "Well, sir, she has been getting on my nerves around the office, so I'm fine with it," he said, only half kidding. "Do you understand what our arrangement is with the parks commission? I mean, we'd have to run it by them if it's what Sandy wants to do."

"Hugh assures me they'll be fine with it. Apparently they're pretty pleased with the job you're doing and aren't worried about her leaving. And my friend Geren Randolph over at our competitor bank will be most happy to have her off his payroll and on to mine. So if you say 'yes' and she accepts, everyone is happy."

Cutter knew full well Sandy would accept. He also knew accepting for her would be a big mistake, and things were going so well right now he didn't want to fuck it up. "I have no problem with it at all. But you'll have to ask her. I might also suggest you never let her know you asked me. You'd be doing us both a favor."

"Agreed." Ty stood and offered his hand across the massive desk. Cutter shook it and looked Ty in the eye. For a brief second he saw something there that gave him a chill, but it was gone so quickly he decided it must have been a trick of the light. Or possibly the dark gray steel he had just looked into.

That afternoon, Cutter and Alan met with the commission and the council. Before they arrived, Alan set up the presentation boards for the commissioners and council members to peruse. Cutter sat on a table at the front of the room as folks showed up and began inspecting Alan's boards. He watched as they gathered in small groups, talking and pointing at this or that illustration. He could hear the tone of questioning in the low murmur of discussions. He counted noses until he was sure a quorum of both bodies was present and then asked folks to take a seat.

"Thanks for taking time to meet with me today," Cutter began, using his best aw-shucks personality.

"Well, Sonny, if you think we're going to give you more money because you drew some pretty pictures, you've kinda wasted yours and our time." This came from Sally Palin, City Council's resident blue-haired misanthrope.

"Why don't you sit down and let the Director have his say?" Ham and Eggs barked. Sally sat. And frowned.

132

Over the next two hours, Cutter explained the project, fielded questions, watched nervously as the two boards separated and held discussions, and finally grinned in relief as both bodies handed him the necessary votes to go forth with making a proposal to the Jacob Matthew Cup and entering into a 30 month lease deal with the Cup organization should their proposal be accepted.

Ham and Eggs offered one last bit of advice. "I think Hugh and I should hold a meeting with the community beforehand so we don't run into the problem they're having in Vail."

"No," Cutter told him. "I want to hold the public meeting. Think about it. If it gets a lead balloon award, it falls on me, not on any of you. You can disavow any knowledge of the idea." Ethan Hunt. All he needed was the self-destructing tape.

Two days later, Cutter announced a community meeting to discuss improvement needs at Riverside Park. He asked Alan and his staff to join him at the meeting. Alan asked "Will the boards we already did be enough or do you want us to do some additional ones?"

"I don't want any boards," Cutter told him. Cutter had learned the surest way to have the community shoot down your plans was to actually show them to the community. Cutter used a format for those meetings which consisted of asking every participant to offer one idea for improvements to a park, in this case Riverside. He would go around the room until every conceivable idea was listed on large sheets of paper and would then give each participant five voting stickers to put on their top five wishes. He would then take those lists back to the planning staff and have them "draw up" the public's plan, which almost always looked exactly like what they had already prepared. But to make sure, Cutter would always salt the audience with folks who made sure all the right ideas were up there.

This was exactly how he handled the public meeting. After all ideas were up and voted on, Cutter outlined the potential for acquiring funding for the improvements by hosting the Jake. By this time, the audience was so excited to see new and improved facilities, it seemed like a small cost to close the park for two and a half years. By an enthusiastic show of hands, the community group endorsed the submission of a proposal. The only reporter in attendance was Ruth Roberts who took many notes, though she knew there would be no article about the meeting. At least not in the immediate future. She was there only to report back to her publisher.

As the meeting ended and the crowd made its way to the parking lot, Cutter was approached by a broad chested man with thick salt and pepper hair and a shaggy moustache. Cutter did a double take. The guy looked exactly like his golfing acquaintance from Fort Myers, Mutt. Of Mutt and Jeff. Cutter liked him immediately, before the guy said a word, purely because he liked Mutt. He found that an odd reaction but went with it.

By way of introduction, Mutt II snapped a business card at Cutter and said, "Bartholomew Jones, constitutional lawyer. Protector of the poor and down trodden.

Poor either before or because I represent them. At your service."

Cutter studied the proffered card. Indeed, it said "Bartholomew A. Jones, Attorney-at Law" right under an image of a black knight chess piece, a horse's head. No address, only a phone number. "What can I do for you, Attorney Jones?"

"Ah. Right question. Wrong order. It's what I can do for you."

"And what might that be?" Cutter wanted to know.

"I believe you will need me to be your lawyer in this venture."

"Why do you think I might need a lawyer, and however do you think I might be able to afford a constitutional lawyer?"

"Walk me to my car and I'll tell you," Jones responded.

As Cutter gathered up his things and made his way with the attorney to the parking lot, Jones (who Cutter would come to find out was called, by almost everyone who knew him, "Black Bart") filled him in. "It appears to me you will be walking a fine line between the public and private sector. The city attorney will represent the city's interests, but if those interests differ from yours, he won't represent you. Which is where I come in. You give me a dollar, I'm on retainer and if you need help, I go to work. I actually do eminent domain and other real estate law, and I am very interested in this idea. I'll volunteer my time and review documents for you as you go along. You know, to offer my unsolicited advice. And to be prepared in case you fuck up. Which public employees always do." He grinned at Cutter.

"Sounds fair," Cutter said and dug a dollar out of his pocket. He shoved it into Black Bart's hand. "You're hired." They reached Bart's car, an upper end Audi. It sensed when the attorney was near and unlocked, lights going on.

Bart turned back to Cutter and said, "You know the difference between an Audi and a porcupine?"

"No…"

"With a porcupine, the pricks are on the outside," and he was gone, leaving Cutter shaking his head and smiling.

TWELVE

By the mid-May deadline, the team had worked overtime to get everything in place and to get the proposal submitted. As promised, Cord had assembled a list of who's who to serve as the local board. Though not one word had appeared in the media, it seemed that everyone in the community knew what was happening. And to date, not one critic had surfaced. It was pretty amazing to Cutter. Everywhere he went someone would come up to him and tell him how great they thought the plan was.

Cutter had spent enough time around politicians to understand when folks were pumping hot air up his ass, but he had to concur with those who lauded his efforts—he in fact had come up with an idea which would change the face of Columbus, Colorado. Probably get him into the history books, at least the local ones. Maybe his wife and Cord had helped a little, and he would be magnanimous. When they gave him the Man of the Year Award, he would remember to recognize their efforts. Along with thanking all the little people who had made it all possible.

With the submission of the proposal, there was nothing to do but wait. So they waited.

Three days before the special election in Vail, Ty called Cutter and Sandy to invite them to his house to watch, via the internet, the results from the election as they were announced. Along with the folks already involved in the project, all 120 of them. A small gathering of Ty's friends. When they arrived at the Carroll mansion, Cord was at the door to usher them in, laying claim to Sandy and turning Cutter over to Beth. Drinks in hand, they joined Ty in front of the giant television screen hooked directly to what appeared to be the Eagle County Clerk's personal election count screen. Which meant that Ty would get the results before any news outlet. Cutter was not surprised.

Ty spied Sandy and immediately led her aside and whispered confidentially to her. Cutter guessed, correctly, Ty was offering Sandy the job of executive director should the bid be awarded to Columbus. He saw Sandy's head bob up and down and a wide smile spread across her face. More head bobbing and they shook hands. Cutter smiled and waited for her to come share her news. He was a little miffed when she first seemed to share it with Cord. In fact, he was pissed. She must realize, at some level, that Cutter had had a hand in this. But when she made her way over to him to tell him, he was able to feign surprise and act excited for her.

They watched the screen as the numbers started appearing. A "Yes" vote meant the Jacob Matthew Cup would NOT be going to Vail. That Vail's undeveloped land would be kept as empty and pristine and unused as it had been. And more importantly that Columbus would be in the running. The initial reports showed the "No's" held a substantial lead. Little by little, that lead narrowed and by ten o'clock the tipping point was passed. Within minutes, an underling materialized at Ty's elbow and whispered in his ear. Ty nodded and the underling handed him a cell phone. Ty held his hand up and everyone went silent.

"Hello…Oh, hi, Lois…Yes…No…Alright…Thank you for the call." Ty hung up, a frown on his face. He stood on a small platform in front of the television. He signaled for Cutter and Sandy to join him, which they did.

"Ladies and gentlemen. That phone call was from Lois Borin. She called to tell us that our bid to host the Jacob Matthew Cup has been accepted." Before he could continue, Ty had to wait for the applause to die down. "Yep, I have to agree it is pretty exciting." He turned to Cutter. "And I want to be the first to congratulate Cutter Williams for his work in bringing this boon to us." More applause. Cutter actually blushed. Christ in a handbasket. This was just too fucking cool. "And I want to let you all know Sandy Williams has accepted our offer to act as the executive director of the local Jake board." More applause. Sandy didn't blush.

Ty turned to Cutter again and said, quietly, "You ready to meet the press?"

Cutter looked confused, but nodded his head.

"Good," Ty told him, "because they are ready to talk to you," and he pointed out the window where a gaggle of reporters had gathered. Cutter couldn't believe it. How had this happened so quickly? It had only been twenty minutes since Ty had gotten the call from Lois. But before he had any time to think about it, Cutter was whisked out the door, where bright lights burst in his eyes and temporarily blinded him. A microphone was shoved in his face, quickly followed by several more.

"Director Williams, we understand you have some exciting news to share with us." This from Laurie Loftus, the most recognizable local news anchor. *Wow, she looks even better in person than she does on TV* was Cutter's sole reaction. What he managed to say was "Uh…uh….uh…"

"Uh?" Laurie asked.

Cutter finally, thankfully, revived. And shared the news with them. Answered their questions, including the one from Ruth Roberts asking who came up with the idea to use Riverside Park. Cutter explained it was his idea, happy he would get credit for this bit of genius. Behind him stood Sandy and Cord, smiling broadly. Next to them was Ty, whose smile was much more subdued, more like the mountain lion which had just eaten the eagle.

The next morning Cutter and Sandy joined Cord for breakfast to review the plans for the next few weeks. As they finished, Cutter told Cord, "Hey, Wild Bill, Sandy had a terrific idea last night. We want you and Beth and the kids to join us on vacation in August. Our treat. We're going to take you to one of our favorite places, the Outer Banks of North Carolina. House on the beach. Nothing to do but relax and sit in the sun. Maybe drink a beer or eight. Just one rule—no phones or computers."

"Lots of beer and no phones? Hmmmm… I suppose we could do that. If you let us buy the beer."

"Deal."

The next two months were a whirlwind of activity for the Williams family. Sandy was working 60 hours a week in addition to traveling frequently to Denver to meet with the Jake staff. Cutter drew most of the parenting chores, including getting Jordan in and out of camps, most of which she shared with Sabri, so she was happy. While most everyone, especially commission and council members, assumed summer was Cutter's busiest season, truth be told, it was his easiest. His work, planning and preparing for the busy season, had to be done by April, or not done at all. His summer work hours this year were spent reviewing architectural and engineering plans for the work to be done in Riverside as well as reviewing and signing the hundreds of legal documents required by all the parties involved in hosting the Jake. What the hell ever happened to sitting down, agreeing to things and sealing it with a handshake? Fucking attorneys.

But Cutter was not so naïve that he didn't have his attorney also review all those papers as well.

Cutter punched Black Bart's number into his cell phone. After the second ring it went to voice mail. "You have reached the cell phone of Bartholomew Jones, constitutional lawyer." As the recorded massage droned on, Cutter's mind wandered, this time to how good Rachel looked this morning. "Press two for Amendment One, press three for Amendment Two, press four..." He knew he shouldn't think about Rachel, at least in that manner, but still. After all, a guy can daydream, can't he? The now irritating message had continued to "Press six" when Cutter was yanked from his reverie with "For god-sakes, Cutter. Are you unconscious or just painfully slow? What do you want?" Cutter looked at his phone, finally comprehending.

"Mr. Jones. So nice of you to take my call. I was wondering if you had a chance to go over the final lease documents."

Bart, using his sonorous courtroom voice, told him, "They seem to all be in order. Funny thing though. I checked with the city attorney and then with the county recorder's office. Nobody seems to have a copy of the deed for Riverside Park. Could you check to see if your office has it? Not really a big deal, but you know how we attorneys are. I's dotted, t's crossed. It's a constitutional thing."

"I'll check," Cutter said and disconnected the call. Waited two minutes and redialed Black Bart. Let Bart get to "Press three" and Cutter pressed and held the '3' button, sending an irritating screech into Bart's ear.

"Dammit, Cutter. What do you want now?"

"What is Amendment Two?"

"Fuck if I know." This time Jones hung up on Cutter, both of them smiling.

Cutter walked out of his office and headed back to Rachel's to ask her to research the deed. Without thinking he wheeled into her office and started to speak, stopped abruptly when he saw she was practically yelling into the phone.

"Listen asshole, one more time. That's it. Just once and I'll have your ass, you..." This time, Rachel stopped abruptly as she saw Cutter. She slammed down the phone and blushed. "Sorry, Cutter. That was personal." She was quiet and gathered herself, then added, "What can I do for you?"

Cutter told her what he needed on the deed issue and asked, "And what can I do for you?"

"Train my asshole husband."

"Uh…"

"Sorry. I'll see what I can find on the deed."

Two hours later, Rachel was at his desk. "Cutter, I'm sorry about earlier. Please forget I said anything. I'm sure the Chief and I will work it out," a sarcastic reference to her husband. "I have not been able to find any copy of a deed for Riverside. Found them for many of our properties, but none for any of the older parks. I'll keep looking."

"Thanks. Let me know if you find anything," wondering about the lack of a deed but distracted by noticing Rachel had been crying. "And let me know if there is anything I can do for you."

"Thanks." And she was gone. Christ in a handbasket.

Cutter returned his attention to the task at hand—finalizing the rental of a beach house in Frisco, North Carolina. He had settled on an older, but large house, right on the beach on Marlin Drive. More space than his family and the Richards family would need, but he wanted something nice to say "thank you" for everything Cord had done for them.

Four weeks later, the two families landed at Norfolk International Airport, picked up their two 4-wheel drive

SUVs and started the three hour drive down to Frisco. Since Sandy wanted to finish up "just a wee bit of business" before they got there, she rode with Cord and the younger children, and Beth and Cutter took Sabrina and Jordan with them. They agreed to meet at the Froggy Dog in Avon for dinner and then stop for supplies at the Food Lion.

As Cutter drove over the causeway into Kitty Hawk, lots of memories flooded back. Island time. Working on the *Debbie Lee*. Finding his way. He wondered if Sandy had the same reaction. A small attack of nostalgia that made him a little reflective. A large assault of sea smell and sun bouncing off the ocean that made him smile. Out of the corner of his eye, he saw Beth staring at him. He turned and said to her, "Old memories. I'm sure you'll tire of hearing them but welcome to the Outer Banks. God's gift to the weary."

That evening, at the door to the beach house, Cutter went around and collected cell phones. Only Sandy complained. Cutter allowed as how they could check their voice mail once in the morning and once in the evening. Only Sandy seemed relieved.

Over the next few days, they had the Hatteras Island experience. That is, they did nothing but eat and drink and play with kids and lie in the sun and eat and drink some more. Cutter did run down to Hatteras Village and checked in with Captain T. Jefferson of the good ship *Debbie Lee*, for old time's sake. He loved seeing his old boss and sailing mate, but after fifteen minutes of talk, they both realized they really didn't have much to say to each other. Another small wave of nostalgia passed quickly.

The wives decided, as mothers are wont to do, that no vacation with kids is so good it can't be ruined with a little cultural education. To that end, they planned a trip with Jordan and Sabrina on Wednesday up to Nags Head/Manteo to visit some educational attractions. Jordan fussed about it ("Mom, why do we have to? That's no fun."), but when Sabri seemed excited about a day trip, Jordan quickly changed her tune.

Wednesday morning, Cutter was dressing to go for a run with Cord when Sandy moaned from their bed, "Cutter, I feel terrible. I think I may have gotten some bad crab last night or something. Would you mind going with Beth and the girls today? I'll owe you one."

Before he could answer, Sandy jumped up and ran into the bathroom. Cutter had been ready to whine his way out of having to go, but he was distracted by Sandy's bouncing bare boobs and naked behind and suddenly felt compelled to agree to her request. By the time Sandy was back in bed pulling the covers over her head, Cutter was changing into shorts and his brand new OBX tee shirt. He patted his wife on the rump and told her to feel better. She grunted in reply.

Half an hour later, he and Beth and the girls were headed up Highway 12, leaving Theano and Livingston with Cord who wondered what the hell had happened to his sitting on the beach, drinking beer with Cutter, with the two babies safely ensconced in a fort dug into the sand. He'd been a good sport about it when Cutter

145

asked but said Cutter would owe him one. Cutter did the math—he got one from Sandy but lost it ten minutes later to Cord. Helluva vacation.

Cutter's group ended up having a terrific time. They visited the aquarium in Manteo (a hit with both girls); toured the Wright Brothers National Memorial (a hit with Beth, but the girls were bored); rolled down the dunes at Jockey's Ridge (a hit with everyone except Beth); played miniature golf, had lunch and ice cream (a hit with everyone). By the time they got to Bonner Bridge, the girls were sound asleep. Sandy met the car as they parked under the house and helped carry Jordan to bed. She thanked Cutter profusely for taking the trip. She even got him a beer and a sandwich on deck while the four grownups watched the sun go down.

The next morning, Cutter again dressed to take a run up to the Frisco Woods campground with Cord and Beth. There was nothing Cutter liked better about vacation than getting to take this four mile run early in the day. It was a lot easier than running in hilly, low oxygen Colorado and meant he could eat and drink whatever he wanted all day without guilt. He cursed under his breath when he realized he had run out of clean socks, so he padded into the bathroom to retrieve a dirty pair from the hamper. When he picked up his wife's underwear, the lacy pink ones he so liked, from the top of the pile of clothes, he clinched in disbelief. He couldn't believe what he felt.

Any male who was ever fourteen and had a sock or handkerchief stuck under his mattress (which is to say every male) knew what that sock felt like after a night of teen fantasy. Sandy's underwear felt exactly the same. How could that be? They hadn't all vacation, though he had tried. Maybe she used it to blow her nose. Maybe he was confused. How? What? Who? Cord? No, that absolutely could not be. There must be some reasonable explanation. It was so ludicrous he couldn't even figure out how to ask Sandy.

"You coming?" Cord yelled up to Cutter.

"Uh. Yeah. Give me a sec."

He found some socks and pulled on his shoes, completely unaware of his surroundings. He joined them outside and the three of them jogged out toward Highway 12. Cutter was seeing nothing, he was feeling nothing. It couldn't be. It can't be. He could look at neither Beth nor Cord. His eyes stung. He could feel his heartbeat in his temples. He tasted bile and thought for a few moments that he might throw up. Impossible. There must be an explanation.

As they ran along 12 north toward the entrance to the campground, Cutter thought about the time Sandy had spent around Cord. They worked together. They always seemed like good friends at parties or family get-togethers. But she never said anything about him. It was the four of them. Never anything untoward. For Christsake, Cord was his best friend. Since Clint. Christ in a handbasket. He should have seen. No, it can't fucking be possible.

"Hey, Cutter, you wanna wait for us? You running the Boston Marathon or something?" Cord yelled. Cutter had started sprinting without thinking. Cutter slowed and tried to answer but no words would form. His eyes started to tear, but the tears blended with the sweat and no one noticed. There must be an explanation. I must be wrong. They made their way into the campground, turned around and started home.

"Cutter, you okay?" Beth asked.

"Fucking perfect," he barked and then realized he had yelled at the wrong person. "Sorry, Beth. I guess I just got up on the wrong side of the bed."

"No problem," she answered, and reached over and squeezed his arm. Which brought on more tears. They jogged home with no further conversation, though Cutter did notice that Cord was eyeing him carefully. They entered Marlin Drive and approached the house. Sandy was at the foot of the stairs to the house, holding both the little ones with Jordan and Sabrina holding onto her legs. Cutter saw immediately that Sandy knew he had discovered what was going on. She was using the kids as a defense.

"Cutter," she started and choked. Tears in her eyes. Bitch, it's too late for that. "Cutter, your brother Jim called. Your dad died this morning."

THIRTEEN

The Right Honorable Carleton Humphrey pushed his oversized leather chair back from his oversized mahogany desk and instructed his perfectly-sized secretary to close the door as she left his office. And he told her he wished not to be disturbed for the remainder of the afternoon. When she was gone, he retrieved a cigar from his credenza, poured himself a bourbon and branch water and lumbered to his couch. He pulled off his lizard skin cowboy boots and rubbed his feet. He sat down and curled his feet up under himself and sat, looking like a gnome, albeit a smug and self-satisfied one.

"Mayor, you are one brilliant son of a bitch," he whispered to himself, though, truth be told, Carleton had never had one original or generous idea in his life. He had just gotten off the phone after talking with Ty Carroll. Ty had told him the Riverside Park problem had been solved. That the mayor should take it off his plate and not worry any more about it. Ty had invited Carleton and his equally dumpy wife to dinner two nights hence. Carleton knew if he played his cards right, the park thing would work itself out. And it had. Time to reap the rewards. The dinner would be the perfect time to seek Ty's support for a run for U.S. Congress.

The dinner went exceptionally well, at least from Carleton's point of view. Ty was chatty and convivial. When the mayor brought up getting support for a run at a new office, Ty suggested they discuss it after dinner. Mrs. Carroll was, as it had become second nature by now, a gracious hostess and charming dinner companion. Especially compared to the not quite as charming Mrs. Humphrey, who not only belched several times during dinner, but had also begged for a third tiny piece of cake. Even so, as they finished coffee (and Mrs. Humphrey her third piece of cake), Mrs. Carroll politely suggested the ladies retire to her sitting room for some "girl talk" and leave the men to their boring business discussion.

As soon as the women left, Carleton launched into his plea for support. "Mr. Carroll, Ty if I may, I would really like to thank you for all you have done for me over the years."

"Think nothing of it," Ty offered.

"But now I would like your support for another office. It is my plan to run for Congress next year and of course your support would be vital to my campaign. Now before you say anything, I understand you are a big supporter of our current Congresswoman, Whitney Husz, but after all, she is in the other party and our party really needs the support in DC right now. I'm sure you can see that. And no one else has put in the time in politics that I have. I've earned this chance. What'da say?"

Ty smiled his enigmatic smile, the one that showed no teeth and was somehow alarming. "I'm sorry, Carleton, I truly am. But there is no way I can help you on that.

You see, tomorrow morning you are scheduled for a press conference at seven-thirty in which you are going to resign from your current position and retire from politics completely."

Without considering it was Ty Carroll he was addressing, Humphrey erupted, "What the bloody hell are you talking about? Why the fuck would I resign? I do a great job. I am great for this city. Are you nuts? I've done everything you have asked and the people love me. You must be crazy if you think I'll leave." By this time, his face was purple and the veins above his too-tight collar were throbbing.

"Please," Ty said quietly, "keep your voice down. At least try to act like an adult. And sit down." Carleton sat, slapping his hand on the table. Ty got up and walked to the bar where he poured two whiskeys and handed the fuller one to the mayor. "Listen, Carleton, you're not going to be thrown out on your butt with nowhere to land." And at the same time thought "Lucky for you I'm being so generous. You wouldn't last a week on your own." He continued, "We've arranged for you to have a position in our real estate firm. As soon as you announce your resignation, your office will be ready for you. Though you might want to take the missus on a little vacation for a couple of weeks. Paid of course."

The mayor sat frowning and said nothing for a few minutes. Finally, he asked, "Why?"

"Well, frankly, you've become an embarrassment. It's time for the City of Columbus to take its place in the upper echelon of the cities of the West. And your blustering and bullying and pandering just won't fit in. Neither will the bootlickers and buffoons you have surrounded yourself with. Time to move on and give someone else a chance."

As soon as it dawned on him his replacement, by law, would be the president of City Council, Hammond Eggleston, the soon-to-be ex-mayor was back on his feet. This time sputtering and practically foaming at the mouth. "I knew it. This is all Eggleston's doing. That low-life mother fucker. I'll have his ass for this."

"Once again, shut up and sit down. Eggleston had nothing to do with this. It's just your time. Man up."

Now it was Humphrey's turn to get very quiet. He glared at Carroll. Finally he said, "You forget, Ty, I know about your plans for Riverside Park. I'm sure you wouldn't want that to get out, now would you?" he smirked.

Ty smiled his mountain lion smile. "Gee, Mr. Mayor, I have no idea what you're talking about. But come to mention it, any public discussion of Riverside would eventually lead to the subject of the young lady who worked for you who met such an untimely end. And your part in that. Think very carefully before you decide to go up that road. So to speak."

Humphrey was slow, but not even he was that slow. He slumped back into his chair and rubbed his bald head with both hands. His fucking idiot brother. Dumbest thing I ever did was hiring that retard. Between him and our stupid sister who can't keep her panties up and married that asshole Eggleston. And now his brother had taken away his only bargaining chip. Son of a bitch.

The day Carleton Humphrey was sworn in as mayor, his first official act was to hire his younger brother, Viceroy, whom the family called Vick. Well, called him Vick until he was in the third grade. Carleton was two years older than Vick, but Vick was much bigger. In fact, by the time he got to third grade, Vick outweighed his older brother by 25 pounds. Outweighed every kid in his own class by at least 30 pounds. Which made their elementary school principal note the Humphreys had gotten their "Cart" before their "Horse". From that day on, everyone, family included, called Vick "Horse." Horse was just dumb enough to think it was a compliment.

If a person were to look up loser in the dictionary, Horse's picture would be right there. He never stopped gaining weight in his life and tipped the scales at 350 pounds. He was lazy and slovenly. He lived with his parents until they died, then lived in their house until the bank foreclosed and threw him out. His brother rented him a small apartment and got him a job as a janitor in a school. A job he kept only because his brother was on council. Finally, Carleton became mayor and hired Horse to be a personal assistant. Horse got to wear a special uniform which, from a distance, looked like a police uniform, complete with badge. But no weapons. His job, his only job, was to run errands for hizzoner.

When the mayor noticed Jean Smith skulking around with her recorder while he was talking to Ty Carroll on the phone, he decided it might be wise to find out exactly what she had recorded. He called his brother up and told him to go get the recorder from Jean. Horse found her just as she was leaving the City Hall Annex and followed her when she drove out of the parking lot, trying to figure out how to stop her. Figuring out was not Horse's strongest suit. He followed her out of the city and up into the mountains. Finally he started honking his horn and flashing his lights. It only made her speed up. So Horse sped up, getting almost close enough to touch her bumper. He saw the curve up ahead. Jean apparently did not. At least in time. She slammed on the brakes but it was too late. She went over the embankment.

Horse stopped and looked over the edge at her car. At least it didn't catch on fire. He knew he would be in trouble, but he had to get the recorder for his brother and had to rescue her. He figured he could claim he had seen someone run her off the road. Over the next 30 minutes, Horse lowered his 350 pounds of fat down the mountainside. There he found Jean dead and despite the below freezing temperatures, he broke into a cold sweat. Decided he would leave her there, unless another car came along and saw his car. He found the recorder, put it in his pocket and spent another 60 minutes hauling his fat ass up the hill. No other cars had passed.

He drove back to City Hall and gave his brother the recorder. When Carleton asked if it had been a problem, Horse told him, "No, I told her you wanted it, and she handed it over." Carleton asked what she had said. Making

154

up one lie was within Horse's wheelhouse. Making up a second was beyond his ken. He told the mayor what had happened. His brother screamed at him and slapped him on the side of the head. Horse was so used to this kind of treatment from Carleton, it didn't bother him. Though he was upset that Carleton didn't appreciate all the effort it had taken to climb up and down the mountain.

Mayor Humphrey stared at Ty and realized he was in a box. Still, he had a few people he needed to pay back for not giving him the respect he thought he deserved. "Okay. I'll resign. But not tomorrow. I need, say, four weeks to finish up my business as mayor."

Ty shook his head. "Sorry. That would be impossible. We can't have you back in your office and give you a chance to muck things up. This offer expires at, well, let's say it is expiring now. In fact," Ty said, looking at his watch, "just about now the police will be finishing up emptying your office. Should I call them and let them know not to take the stuff to your new office at the real estate company? Tell them instead to drop the boxes in front of your house?" He smiled.

"But, but...That's not fair. You can't do that," Humphrey sputtered.

"Done. And done. Now, can I get you another drink?" The smile never left Ty's face.

Indeed, exactly at that time, two police officers were carting the last of the boxes filled with all of the mayor's personal property out of the mayor's office. The detective in charge was making one last sweep of the room

155

and called the chief of police to report that they had finished the job just as the chief had instructed. As he signed off, Detective First Class Ken Dunn made one final check of the mayor's oversize mahogany desk, leaving only paper clips and rubber bands but taking from the bottom drawer a small recorder they had overlooked earlier. Ken slipped it into his jacket pocket and locked the door as he left.

He couldn't remember the last time he had enjoyed an assignment quite as much. It would be so good to see that blowhard Humphrey get dumped on his ass. By the time he got to the van downstairs, he had forgotten all about the recorder, and it remained in the jacket pocket until the next time he wore it, two months later.

The next morning, with all the local electronic media in attendance, Mayor Carleton Humphrey, with his wife and his brother at his side, resigned from office "to pursue other opportunities and to spend more time with my family." He took no questions and left the podium. With Laurie Loftus in hot pursuit, yelling questions at his back. The rest of the media was more interested in the second act of the show, the swearing in of the new mayor, Hammond Eggleston. Laurie's coverage of the event drew the most viewers. What everyone remembered was her playing an old Eagles' song with the footage of ex-mayor Humphrey walking away, head bowed, wife in tow. Laurie had chosen the song *New Kid in Town*, though the only words her audience heard were "They will never forget you 'til somebody new comes along."

When Detective Dunn did find the recorder, he couldn't remember where it came from or how it got there, but it did have a name and address on it, so he threw it into an envelope for his secretary to send out. The next day it was mailed to Jean Smith at her address north of the city, but since Jean was in fact dead, her former life partner, Suzie Morgan, got the package. When she saw the package in her mailbox, it gave her a jolt. When she opened it, it brought back memories. Jean and her stupid recorder. Then Suzie remembered a reporter had had an interest in the thing if it ever showed up. Suzie listened to all of the recordings, and they were all boring and meaningless to her. But that reporter might pay for it.

"Ms. Roberts? This is Suzie Morgan. Do you remember me?"

"I'm sorry," Ruth said, "I talk to a lot of people. I'm afraid I don't remember you."

Asshole reporters, Suzie thought, but told her, "I was Jean Smith's roommate. You gave me your number once and said I should call you if Jean's recorder ever showed up. Well, it came in the mail today, and I was wondering if you still want it."

"I would certainly like the opportunity to listen to it," Ruth told her, remembering how she had obsessed over not being able to hear what Jean had recorded, though she was positive it would contain nothing of any real value. Especially now that Carleton Humphrey was history. Still, she felt that little pang that a reporter gets from not turning over the rock and therefore not knowing.

"How much will you pay?" Suzie asked.

"Pay? I won't pay anything. The *Columbus City Times* does not pay for news."

"Fine. Goodbye." With that Suzie hung up.

Ruth stared at her phone. Dammit. Dammit to hell. She hit the redial button.

"How much?" was how Suzie answered the phone.

"Depends on what is on the recording," Ruth answered.

"Look," Suzie said, summoning her inner most bitch. "I don't know and I don't care what is on the damn thing. If you would like to buy a perfectly good recorder and take your chances, the price is $250."

Ruth thought about it and finally agreed, realizing she would have to pay for it herself. She set up a time and place to make the purchase but made a little mental note to figure out a way to extract $250 worth of revenge from this bitch.

When she finally listened to the recording, which did indeed turn out to be Mayor Humphrey talking to someone on the phone about Riverside Park, she still had no idea what was going on. She realized that Jean had been right. Something was amiss about the conversation. She called Humphrey, but he did not return her calls. Ruth decided the next place to try would be Parks Director Williams. Humphrey's strange call had happened before Williams had arrived on the scene, but maybe he knew something. The big problem was that whomever Humphrey was talking with made Humphrey nervous. You could hear it in his voice. Which meant

158

that it might possibly be her big boss, Ty Carroll. And Director Williams seemed to be a favorite of Ty's. A real potential minefield.

FOURTEEN

Cutter sat at the gate in O'Hare waiting for his flight to the Quad Cities. He always hated having to fly home through this airport. Since the flight was a 30 minute regional jump, it meant that if traffic out of O'Hare got delayed, the regional flights were pushed to the bottom of the priority list. Like this afternoon, when the late August humidity and heat had grown thunderheads to some 60,000 feet and caused some serious storms. He rechecked the flight status board and saw his plane had been delayed yet another 90 minutes. Hell, I could walk home from here in 90 minutes. He called his brother Jim to update him on his arrival time.

Cutter was numb. It was one of those days where incoming information had overloaded the circuits and popped the breaker. First the discovery Sandy might be having an affair, and it might be with his best friend Cord, a realization which coursed through his body and almost strangled him. But before he could step back and regain his breath, the news his father had died. He had called his office to explain about his father and that he would be taking more time off and was told Mayor Humphrey had unexpectedly just resigned. He went into shutdown. He sat looking out the window at planes landing and taking off and not seeing, not hearing, not feeling anything.

Sandy had driven him from the beach house in Frisco to the airport in Norfolk. She tried to talk to him about his dad. He couldn't even look at her. In fact, the only time he even acknowledged her presence was at the airport when she told him they would close up the beach house and join him in Davenport the following evening and that she loved him. His complete response was "Sure." He walked into the terminal without looking back.

His flight was finally called, and the small propjet took off in the rain. The short hop was the bumpiest he could remember. Ordinarily he would have had a death grip on the seat arms and his eyes slammed shut, but he didn't notice until the woman in the business suit seated next to him grabbed his arm and squeezed it so hard he found huge bruises on it the next day. The pain drew him out of his coma, and he patted her hands and told her it would be all right. Though he didn't really know if it would. Nor care, for that matter. Only when the plane stopped bouncing on the tarmac did she release her death grip. She said, "Thank you," without looking at him and was on her feet before the plane got to the gate.

Jim was waiting for him in the terminal. When Cutter saw him, tears filled his eyes. He grabbed his brother and hugged him tightly. Jim patted him on the back. After a couple of minutes, they headed to the parking lot. Cutter asked, "What happened to Dad? I thought he was in good health."

Jim shook his head and told Cutter, "You know, Win, as far as anyone could tell, he was fine. He ate right, got exercise and got annual checkups. I guess it was just one of those things. He sat down with Mom at breakfast, looked out the window, turned to her and said 'Looks like it's going to be a really fine day.' Then he laid his head down next to his plate of scrambled eggs and died. Massive stroke. He was smiling." He paused, then asked, "You okay?"

"Shell-shocked, I guess. How's Mom?"

"Doing really well, actually. Pretty much everyone is at the house. Brother John and his wife Becky were at a conference in Seattle, but they get in tomorrow. The funeral mass is Monday. Dad always said he didn't want one, but you know how Mom is. She had to get him into church just one more time. No eulogy, though. A few prayers and into the family plot at the church. We thought maybe all eight of us kids could be pallbearers. We did decide to have everyone over to the house afterwards for food and memories. And liquor. I think Dad would be okay with that. Though he'd hate thinking he missed a good party."

"Sounds perfect," Cutter told him and then lapsed into silence, thinking about his dad and mom and then about his kids and their mom. They drove the remainder of the way home in their own memories.

Cutter picked his family up at the airport the next evening and was not the least bit surprised to see Cord and Beth had come as well to pay their respects. All Cutter could think was he wished Cord could respect him some. They stopped by the house to greet the family and then checked into the casino hotel in Bettendorf. The two families went to dinner and Cutter spent the entire time looking for some silent communication between Sandy and Cord. He saw none. Later in the hotel, as Sandy went through her nightly ritual in the bathroom, Cutter dug her phone out of her purse. He scrolled through her text messages. He hated himself for doing it and hated even more the message from Cord to Sandy that read "u think C nos bout us?" and her response of "No. He couldn't."

All the next day, Cutter seemed to want to be left alone. They obliged. Except for Jordan, who was not only upset about her grandfather dying but also sensed daddy was feeling very bad so she clung to him. He clung back.

Monday morning, they gathered at the church. A requiem mass is somber and graciously short. One hymn, for Mom Williams and no other extras. At the time the eulogy would normally be delivered, the priest walked to the communion rail and told the mourners, "The family has asked for no eulogy in keeping with Henry's wishes. I would be remiss if I didn't tell you all this. Henry Williams took care of himself, his wife and children, his family and friends, his church and his community, and he did it with a great sense of humor and wonder. No man could do better. Think of him often." The priest turned to finish the mass. Several people cried quietly.

As the last mourners left the church to walk to the nearby gravesite, the eight Williams children gathered

163

around Dad's casket to say good-bye one last time. With no prior discussion, but because Dad had done a similar thing when Grandpa Williams had died, each had brought a small token for their father to take to eternity with him. There was a golf club because Dad had been such a shitty golfer, and John thought he might get a chance to practice in the afterlife. There was a deck of cards for poker. A handkerchief to wipe off windshields and headlights. A chess set, because Dad's chess game was as good as his golf game. A detective book. A ten dollar bill since Dad always claimed you should have a little spending money in your pocket. Dad's goofy hunting hat which he never wore hunting. Cutter placed a champagne flute next to his father's left hand. His sister Patti gave him a quizzical look and Cutter only smiled.

Back at the house, folks milled around quietly talking, sharing memories and waiting for the food to be brought out. More importantly, for the alcohol to be brought out. Jim and his wife enlisted help from the nieces and nephews, and soon food appeared on every table in the house, including end tables. Two bars were set up. Cutter watched all this from his seat on the stairs with Jordan on his lap. As everyone loaded a plate and got a drink, John stood and told a story about Dad trying to teach him to bowl, a story Cutter had not heard. Tad followed it with a rendition of a story they all knew, "Dad drank too much beer and mowed down Mom's flower bed and then he had to sleep on the dining room floor." Patti looked around until she saw Cutter and asked, "Tell us about the champagne flute you put in with Dad."

Cutter smiled. "When I was around ten years old, we had this great Christmas. It had gotten extremely cold in early December and all the ponds and creeks were frozen over, the kind of freezing which left the ice like perfect glass surfaces. No snow though until a week before Christmas. Then it snowed maybe ten inches or a foot. Christmas Eve, it snowed another two inches, a light fluffy snow which sparkled in the early Christmas morning sun. It was the perfect Christmas snow. The family went to mass, then home for presents and breakfast.

"After breakfast, we all bundled up and piled into the station wagon. I remember we each got to take one new toy with us. As we did every Christmas afternoon, we went to Grandpa and Grandma Williams' farm for round two of the Great American Christmas, right down to the turkey and stuffing and pumpkin pie dinner. Grandpa had cleared all the snow off the pond for us to ice skate. As we sat pulling on our skates, it began to snow again, this time huge flakes which seemed to float in the air. With the very tall pine trees laden with snow icing and the bright red barn as backdrops, it was all so beautiful and nice. Even as a ten year old kid, I knew Christmas just didn't get any better.

"Anyway, as we skated around, I saw Dad sitting on the dock with this humongous grin on his face. I skated over and plopped down beside him and asked him what was so funny. I was pretty sure he was going to say something about Chris falling on his ass so much.

Instead, he looked at me and told me life had more than a few perfect moments, but we rarely realized it until well after the fact. But this was one of those moments when we could actually realize it. The snow was perfect, the setting was perfect, everyone in the family was there and happy, and more food and more presents awaited us. Then he handed me his champagne flute half full of mimosa and asked if I wanted a drink. Of course I did. Not every day a kid got champagne. I drained the glass and watched you all skating around. I handed him the empty glass, and he gave it back to me and said, 'Win, you keep this glass to help you remember this perfect moment.' I kept it. Still have it at home. I thought maybe he would like to have one to help him remember the perfect moments."

Only then did Cutter notice everyone was looking at him. He looked across the room and saw Sandy, sitting next to Cord, a tear running down her cheek. And Cutter knew he would never have another perfect moment in his life.

FIFTEEN

On Thursday two and a half weeks later, Cutter sat at his desk and stared into space. He had stayed around Davenport for another week after the funeral to help his baby sister Cathy Rose and her husband Phil sort through all of Dad's belongings so Mom didn't have to do it. Mostly Cutter had volunteered for the task because he didn't want to return to Colorado with Sandy and the kids. He had needed time to think, though that proved to be a fruitless activity.

Immediately after he returned, he had to attend the groundbreaking ceremony for facilities in Riverside Park for the Jacob Matthew Cup. While he was in Davenport, the community had a huge "Riverside Rocks Festival" to mark its closing for construction. Everyone agreed they would miss having the park for two and a half years, but in the long run, it would be worth it. Cutter declined to speak at the groundbreaking. He was surprised to find Sandy had agreed to talk and peppered her speech with lots of references to him and how he had come up with this grand idea. At the end of the event, the newly-minted mayor, Hammond Eggleston, pulled Cutter aside.

"Son," Ham and Eggs smiled, "I need for you to start attending my cabinet meetings."

Cutter shook his head. "Mr. Mayor, you know…"

"Ham and Eggs, Son, Ham and Eggs! Nothing has changed," the mayor interrupted.

"Well, sir, you know how I feel about those meetings. They're a waste of time."

"They won't be. I promise no more than an hour a week. Only the other directors will be there. You need to go because you are going to need those folks' support for your event. Traffic, police and fire, sanitation, development. They are all going to have a role in this and you need to be able to tell them what to do."

Cutter looked at the new mayor and saw he was dead serious. For the first time since the beach, Cutter actually grinned. "Yessir. I'll be there."

"Great. Now let's go grab some lunch and a beer. My treat." Mayor Ham and Eggs spun and quickly walked away, catching his police bodyguard by such surprise she had to run to catch up. "Meet you at the Aspen in twenty minutes," the mayor yelled over his shoulder.

But Cutter could not come out of his funk. He was overcome by inertia. When he wasn't thinking about his wife, he was thinking about his dad. Or worrying about his mom. Or his kids. He had lost all interest in his job and the Jake. The following week Sandy had to go to Denver for yet more meetings, three days' worth. On Wednesday night, Sandy called and talked to Jordan and Livingston. When she asked to talk to Cutter he said he would call her back in a few. He put the kids to bed and, instead of calling Sandy's cell phone, he called her hotel and asked for her room. The desk clerk kindly told him that no Sandy Williams was registered. He looked at the phone and heard the clerk ask if there was anything else he could do. Cutter asked if Cord Richards was registered and was told yes. Cutter hung up and turned off his cell phone. He drank himself to sleep by 3:00 a.m.

The next day, exactly three weeks to the day after his life had started to crash, he sat at his desk and stared, red eyed, into space. Rachel Red Cloud walked into his office and sat on the couch and looked at him. Cutter said nothing. She watched him for a few minutes and then told him, "Director, I realize you just lost your dad and that has to be very difficult, but you need to come back to us. You have answered every question in the last two weeks with 'Yes,' 'No,' or 'Can't you handle it yourself?' You look like crap. We're all concerned about you. What can we do to help?"

"I don't think there's a thing you can do. But I appreciate your asking." He paused, then added, "You're right, you know. I have been somewhere else." Cutter looked at her and thought for a minute. "On second thought, you could do me a big favor. Sandy gets back from Denver this evening, and I have to pick up the kids and feed them before she arrives. If you aren't doing anything, could you possibly take care of them until she gets home?"

Rachel looked a little surprised but nodded and said, "Sure. I guess so."

169

A little animation surfaced in Cutter's face. "Thanks. That would be terrific. I'll owe you a big one. And if you want to take your daughter over to meet my kids, that would be fine. In fact, I'm sure Jordan would love to be around a big girl for a few hours."

They made the arrangements. As Rachel left to pick up her daughter and then Cutter's children, she asked, "When should I tell Sandy you'll be home?"

"If she asks, just say you don't know."

As soon as she had gone, Cutter drove home and packed a bag with a few days' worth of clothes. He drove downtown and got a room at the Founders Hotel. He put his stuff away in his room, turned off his cell phone, put it in a drawer and walked the five flights down to the basement bar and had two airplane gin and tonics. He realized he was famished and decided to treat himself to prime rib, which he found one story up in the hotel's upscale restaurant, The Pioneer. He ordered his prime rib the way Amanda had taught him, all those years ago: if it's frozen, thaw it; if it's thawed, serve it. After dinner, he went back to the basement bar, watched Denver stomp Chicago on Thursday night football and drank enough bourbon that he did not remember getting to his room.

The next morning, he called Alicia and told her he would be back to work on Monday, some time. Instructed her to tell Rachel she was in charge. He drove to the South Mt. Elbert Trailhead north of town and hiked up the mountain for his first 14. By the time he reached the peak he had a splitting headache and couldn't focus his eyes, but for the first time in what seemed forever, he felt alive. He made a very slow descent and got back to his car at sundown. He drove to Leadville and checked into the Doc Holliday room in the Delaware Hotel. In honor of John Wayne and Jimmy Buffett, he had a few beers.

Saturday morning, he got up early, had coffee and breakfast and wandered around town. The fog in his soul had lifted, and he decided what he had to do. He turned his phone back on and saw he had half dozen missed calls, four from Sandy, one from Cord and one final one from the mayor. Without listening, he erased all the voice mails except Eggleston's. Ham and Eggs' message said that Sandy had called looking for him. He erased that message as well. He spent the night again in Doc's room and despite the claims the hotel made, he did not see Doc's ghost.

Sunday morning he drove back to Columbus and got home while Sandy and the kids were at church. He was waiting on them when they got home. Jordan squealed and hugged him and Livingston crawled in his lap. Sandy was not as welcoming.

"Where have you been?" she demanded. Cutter had seen this look and heard this tone of voice only twice in all the time he had known his wife. Once was when a music teacher made the mistake of telling Jordan to just mouth the words because she was making the other kids sing off key. The music teacher was lucky to escape with her job intact. Her self-confidence wasn't as lucky. The other time was when she gutted and fileted Clint

Brandsgard like a rainbow trout. He wasn't as lucky as the music teacher.

"Out." It was Cutter's total response.

Cutter played with the kids for a while, listened to Jordan's stories and fixed them lunch. Sandy had disappeared upstairs. After lunch, he put Livingston down for his nap and plopped Jordan in front of her favorite video. He went upstairs to find Sandy. She was in bed and it was obvious she had been crying.

"I'm so sorry, Cutter. I didn't mean for this to happen."

"How could you?" was all he could think to ask.

"You know, Winston, sometimes you remind me of the guy who was walking through the woods on a cold winter morning. He's kicking his way through the snow and all of a sudden he hears this little voice saying, 'Help me. Please help me.' He looks around and sees no one, so he starts to walk on. Again this desperate little voice says, 'Oh, please sir, save me.' The guy stops again and kicks at the snow and sees a snake lying in the snow, freezing to death. The guy jumps back and says, 'I can't help you. You're a snake. You would bite me,' and the snake says, 'Please pick me up and warm me and I won't hurt you.' So the guy is overcome with pity and he picks up the snake and puts it in his pocket and walks on. Pretty soon, the snake gets all warmed up and bites the guy on the leg. The guy grabs the snake out of his pocket and throws it on the ground and says, 'I thought you said if I saved you, you wouldn't hurt me.' The snake looks at him and says. 'Hey mister, you knew I was a snake when you picked me up'."

Sandy was trying to shift some small part of responsibility for their situation onto Cutter, but she knew she was really just trying to make herself feel less shitty. Sandy was very smart and on occasion, introspective enough to know that she had father issues. Her father cherished Sandy's athlete brothers and pretty much relegated Sandy to a support role. She was a female and as such, her lot was to be mommy's helper in the kitchen until she was old enough to get her own husband. Sandy's dad was never mean to her. He just gave her no affection. But the knowledge didn't help Sandy deal with her feelings. She always knew she was the smartest and most deserving person in the room. If she wanted something, she believed she had every right to have it.

Before she even met Cord Richards, the day Beth described how good he was in bed, she started thinking about him. When the two of them were skiing with their weaker mates lounging in the lodge, she was thrilled with the way he attacked the mountain. Not one ounce of anything but male in his being. At the end of the day, he challenged her to keep up with him on the toughest run on the mountain. She did and when they reached the bottom, he grabbed her and pulled her in and kissed her. Kissed her as if it were his natural right. She felt his excitement through the bulk of both of their ski pants. And felt her own insides weaken for him. The next day, every run ended in much the same way. Within a week, they were in bed. And it was better than she could have ever guessed any sex could be.

Cord figured out a way for them to spend much of their days together. She had met him in Denver for three days and during their bedroom marathon, he told her about the Jacob Matthew Cup and how Columbus might be able to get it. If they could get it, Ty would hire her to work with Cord on it. But because Ty wanted it to come from a public figure, she would have to convince Cutter to take on the project. Oh, and to use Riverside Park for it. She really didn't want Cutter, or her kids, involved in this mess she was getting herself into, but when this incredible male took her places she had never even imagined, she agreed. For the first time in her life, she did not mind being subservient to a man.

The guilt had grown. It had gotten more and more difficult to hide. She made every effort to continue to have sex with Cutter and act as if things were the same. But they weren't. She found herself wishing Cutter, and Beth, would disappear from the planet. Or run off together. But when she was at work with Cord, or wherever she was with him, she forgot all the guilt.

Cutter asked her, "What happens now? Is it over? Do you want a divorce? Do you want me to just take the kids and leave?"

Sandy was stunned. Speechless. Never did she even consider she might be separated from her children. What the hell was Cutter saying? Was he threatening her? Well, fuck him.

"No. I'll end it," she said quietly. Her head meant it when she said it. In her gut, she knew she was lying to both Cutter and herself.

During the next three weeks, Cutter was a person he didn't want to be. He spied on Sandy, checked her emails and phone messages and tried to track where she was all the time. Every day it pissed her off more. Finally, she figured if he wasn't going to trust her, she would go ahead and do what she wanted to. Even though she realized she had done not one thing to earn his trust. It's his fault; he drove me to this. And with that, she was back in bed with Cord. Who was as good as ever, maybe better.

The following day, Sandy picked up the kids and went home. Cutter was not there and did not show up by dinner time. She finally checked in the bedroom and found the note he had left, saying he was moving into an apartment and would pick the kids up on Saturday morning for the day. She should have them ready by 9:00 and he would have them home in time for dinner. And if she had anything she needed him to know, she should leave a message with Alicia.

They started their life apart.

The day Cutter moved into his apartment, conveniently located over the Aspen Ridge Brewery, Detective Ken Dunn found a recorder in his jacket pocket and mailed it to the address taped to it. Within a week, it was in the hands of Ruth Roberts and within days of that, she showed up at Cutter's office and asked to see him.

"What can I do for you?" Cutter asked her after Alicia had shown her in.

Ruth thought for a moment about how to proceed. "Director Williams, can we go off the record for a few minutes? I mean, off the record on both sides. Unless we both agree otherwise, what we say stays between us? Can you do that?"

Cutter tried to remember if he had ever heard a reporter ask for her comments to be confidential. He couldn't. In fact, he found it downright strange. He smiled, nodded his head and replied, "Sure."

Ruth laid a recorder on Cutter's desk and said, "Two years ago, I got a call from a woman who worked in the mayor's office. She told me she had recorded Mayor Humphrey on a phone call, and I needed to listen to the recording. Understand, this woman was a real flake, but you know how we reporters are. I agreed to meet her and hear what she had."

"And this is the recording? Why are you bringing it to me two years later? I wasn't even around two years ago."

"The story got a little strange after she called me. Jean, her name was Jean Smith, died in a traffic accident that night and the recorder disappeared for two years. No one could find it. Then just as mysteriously, it turned up last week. I finally got my hands on it."

"Where was it?" Cutter wanted to know. He loved a good mystery.

"I don't know. But I want you to listen to it and tell me what you think. Off the record, of course."

"Okay." Now he really wanted to hear what was on the recording.

Ruth hit the play button. The machine was obviously cheap and the sound quality not good, but Cutter could make out that jackass Humphrey's voice.

"Yes, Sir. I do understand. I just need a little more time...Why? Because I don't control the damn parks, that's why...I know. That's what I'm trying to do...Yes sir, I do know how urgent it is...Well (unintelligible) asshole (unintelligible) won't listen to reason. Believe me. I will get control of Riverside and it will be closed...For as long as you need it closed, that's how long...Soon. I can't give you a date...You can trust me...Wait, hold on, there's someone outside my door..." The recording ended.

Cutter looked at her and raised his eyebrows, nodding.

"Well?" she asked. "What do you think?"

"I'm not sure. Humphrey never said a word about Riverside to me. In fact, you were the only one whoever mentioned it. Who do you think he was talking to?"

"I don't know. In fact, I'm not sure I want to know. But do you think it has anything to do with what's going on now?"

Cutter thought for a minute. "Beats me. Why would anyone want the park closed? Why would a mayor want to do that? And it's not really closed now. Just shut down for renovation and construction. Did you talk to Humphrey?"

"He won't take my calls. I went to his office, and he sent word out he didn't have to talk to me anymore and in fact, if I wanted a quote, it would be 'Screw you'."

Ruth shook her head slowly. "Well, if you think of anything, let me know."

Cutter smiled his aw-shucks smile and rose to walk her to the door. "You bet. You too, if you figure it all out. If there is anything to figure out." He shook her hand and closed his door after her. Only then did he scowl. Christ in a handbasket. What the fuck was that all about?

SIXTEEN

Cutter missed his kids. He saw them every Saturday and managed to pick Jordan up after school once or twice a week and then get Livingston for a couple of hours, but what he missed most was them both climbing in his lap for pre-bed story time and making them breakfast. He had been out of the house for about three weeks when Jordan asked him when he was coming home.

"That depends, kiddo. You'll have to ask your mom. It's kinda up to her," he told her.

"Mommy says it's up to you and that you're being an asshole."

Cutter couldn't help but smile. "Well, let's just say mom and I have a difference of opinion we have to work out."

Jordan summoned her adult inner self and told him, or more correctly ordered him, "Well, get it worked out before Christmas," and then reverting to the little girl she really was, "Please, Daddy. Please."

The second week in November winter officially descended on Columbus, Colorado. The temperatures dropped dramatically and within days there was two feet of snow on the ground. Cutter and Rachel sat in his office working through the final details of the budget the department was going to submit. Ham and Eggs had promised them a substantial restoration of their operating budget if they could make the case in a presentation to council. Somehow the gurus in the Office of Budget and Management had completely overlooked the fact the department would experience a huge savings from not having to operate its largest park, so it could be a double windfall. Looked like Cutter and company were going to be rolling in the dough. Rachel walked around with a permanent smile stenciled on her face.

They were just finishing up the last of the council presentation when Cutter's door opened hard enough that it banged against the wall and slammed back shut. They both jumped. The door opened more slowly the second time and Beth Richards roared into the office. "Why the hell didn't you tell me what was going on?" she yelled at Cutter, looking at but through Rachel as if she were not there. "You asshole, you knew and let me find out on the street? So both you and that bitch you're married to turn out to be shits." Beth finally took a breath.

Cutter wasn't sure how she did it, but Rachel seemed to fade into the background and disappear from the room. Good. This was hard enough without having her hear it all. "Beth, I am so sorry. I thought you knew. And I sure didn't want to be the one to tell you. How did you find out?"

"The same way I did when this happened before. Cord is well known in town. Eventually someone sees him and it gets back to me."

Cutter asked, "So what are you going to do?"

Beth shook her head and began crying. Finally she calmed enough to sniffle, "What can I do. Whine and cry and bitch at him. Make his life as miserable as possible, though I doubt he'll care. I just can't take the kids and leave. We have no place to go." Cutter walked over and held her. "What are you going to do?" she asked into his chest.

He thought for a minute and told her, "I really don't know." He released her, giving her a tight squeeze before he did. "Why don't I buy you some lunch? And a stiff drink?"

"Sure. If you'll take me to Bradford Q's place. Maybe that will get back to Cord."

It didn't have to get back to Cord. He and Sandy were already there having lunch. Cord ignored them; Sandy glared at Cutter. Cutter made a big deal of kissing Beth on the cheek, taking her coat and holding out her chair. He waved at Sandy, then sauntered over to say hi. Kissed his wife's cheek and patted her shoulder. Cord stood, twisted the end of his moustache and held out his hand to Cutter. Cutter ignored him. Rejoined Beth and ordered them each a double gimlet, up. Cutter noticed Sandy kept giving them the evil eye. They waited until Cord and Sandy left. The tension eased and they both felt better.

After lunch, since he was already downtown, Cutter stopped by the office of his favorite constitutional lawyer, Black Bart Jones. The recording Ruth Roberts had played for him kept nosing its way into his thoughts. He couldn't put his finger on it, but it ate at him, at least

181

when he wasn't worrying about his home life. He had told Ruth he wouldn't share what he had heard but figured he could have a conversation with Jones, and it would be covered by attorney-client privilege. No harm in that, right?

Cutter had no sooner taken a seat in the waiting room than Jones strode in, bellowing, "Someone start the clock. If I have to talk to this guy, at least he's gonna have to pay for it. Through the nose." He reached Cutter and shook his hand. "So what's your constitutional crisis today, Director Williams? Somebody take your *pistola* away? Force you to quarter some G.I. Joes? If they're refusing to serve you drinks, it's not because of the Eighteenth Amendment. That was repealed. It's probably because you're an unpleasant drunk."

"Well, then, never mind." Cutter smiled and walked to the door.

"Come on back. I think it's almost the office cocktail hour," Jones told him as he headed toward his office. Cutter laughed and followed him back.

"So to what do I owe the honor of your presence today?"

"I heard the oddest conversation and thought you might be able to help me sort it out," and he told Bart about the recording and what was on it. The only thing he omitted was who shared it with him. Which was, of course, the first thing Attorney Jones wanted to know. "Sorry, I can't share that part, at least right now. But what do you make of it?"

Bart turned to his credenza, took out a bottle of scotch and poured them each a couple of fingers. "Ice?" Cutter nodded. Bart thought for a while. "Keep in mind, I do real estate law so I would always tend to see things from that perspective. I can think of a few reasons someone would want a park that big and important closed. Someone buying real estate, if they wanted to lower prices in the area around a park, could benefit. The Riverside Park area is the most expensive in the western half of Colorado. If the park was closed long enough and became unkempt, it would drive prices down. Speculators could swoop in, grab property cheap and then get the park restored.

"A developer might also want to lower land values around the park to drive up the value of new development in another area of town. Especially if some new development included recreational features. I would bet there are several of those sorts of people among the mayor's donors. Maybe get that list and start checking around. What would the mayor get out of it? Payoff? The chance to participate?"

Cutter nodded and considered what Bart had told him. "You think since he couldn't get it closed, maybe that's why he resigned? Or maybe he was forced out?"

Bart took another drink, rolled the warm liquor around in his mouth and nodded his head. "Maybe. Seems like a lot of *ifs* and *buts* to spend time or money on trying to figure out. And you know what my momma said about *ifs* and *buts*." Cutter shook his head. "If *ifs* and *buts* were candy and nuts, we'd all have a merry fucking Christmas."

He added, "I'll think on it some. Let you know when I have another brilliant idea."

Cutter grinned and rose to leave. "I won't hold my breath." They both laughed and Cutter let himself out.

The next week, Cutter visited the offices of the local planning and design firm which was helping with the Jake construction. One whole office was filled with plans and pictures and models for the Jake. Cutter was astonished to see the perspectives for the main street area to be built along the river, right in the middle of the park. The last time he had seen any plans, they called for inexpensive buildings with facades designed to make the area look like an alpine village. These plans were for more substantial construction and built to resemble a frontier mining town. In fact, he noticed old photographs of a real town which appeared to be the model for what was being designed.

He asked about the redesign. One of the interns told him an anonymous donor had apparently given big bucks to fast track a new design to be modeled after photos of the original Columbus, Colorado mining town, the one burned down and turned into Riverside Park. He also told him the buildings were being upgraded, again paid for by an anonymous donor. Cutter's first reaction was it was a pretty spectacular idea, perfect in fact. Though he might not want to keep all those buildings in his park. His second thought concerned Bart's theory about closing the park. Except this was IN the park. How could that help any developer? He decided he had to find out if someone was buying up property around Riverside.

Sandy called Cutter to ask if he would come to Thanksgiving dinner at home. He told her, "Depends. Did you end it with Cord?" When she gave a bullshit answer, he declined the invitation. Decided then and there to go to Davenport and spend Thanksgiving with whichever sibling was hosting--if he could wrangle an invitation. Turned out Patti was hosting (thank God, thought Cutter, since Patti is the only real cook in the bunch), so he called her and invited himself. When she told him they were more than welcome, he had to tell her it would just be him. It took Patti not three seconds to figure it out, but she said nothing other than, "Okay. See you next Wednesday." It's the kind of girl his older sister was.

Before he boarded the very expensive flight, he came up with a cock and bull story to explain his coming alone, something to the effect Sandy and the kids were going to a friend's house for Thanksgiving since Sandy had to work on Friday and Saturday. Cutter decided to come because he wanted to make sure Mom was doing okay this first big family holiday after Dad died. Since everyone in the family, except for one nosey sister-in-law, kept their own counsel and would be polite enough not to press the issue, he knew it would pass muster.

His sister Patti picked him up at the airport and for once brought none of her four kids with her. Cutter figured she wanted to give him a chance to talk if he so desired. He didn't but it was such a nice effort, he

185

explained in the simplest terms he and Sandy were separated for a while to work out some problems.

"She has another man, eh?" Patti guessed.

Cutter just shook his head, pretty surprised his sister could see through him that well. "She does, but there must be something wrong with us if it has come to that," he answered.

"Don't count on it," she said. "Sometimes it's just another man." They rode the rest of the way to her house in silence, but Cutter felt more at ease.

The Williams Thanksgiving dinner was served in the late afternoon, so Cutter volunteered to help with kid duty, an effort to get all the grandchildren out from underfoot during food preparation. Kid duty was actually pretty easy, since several years before one of the uncles had hit on the idea of taking all the kids to Miller Time, Davenport's cornucopia of guy stuff—bowling, billiards, video games, sports on huge TVs and a bar which ran from one end of the building to the other. They could set up the kids on an alley or pool table, grab some beers and relax. The kids loved it, the uncles loved it, everyone was happy. Except the moms of course. They didn't think it was fair and complained. Which invariably got them bigger Christmas presents a month later.

Cutter shot a few games of pool and lost ten dollars to Jim, then told everyone he would meet them at the house later. He drove to the family church and walked back to the cemetery to visit his dad's grave. The weather was turning raw, temperatures dropping into the low 30s and growing windy. He found the grave and sat lotus style on the ground at the foot of it. Stared at the headstone. He turned the collar of his pea coat up to keep out the cold. Sat for a long time, thinking about his dad, about growing up with his brothers and sisters, about how families like that worked so well. Wondered about how he screwed up so much with his little family.

Finally, he spoke to his father. "So, Dad, what do I do? How do I fix this? I sure wish you were here to ask." He listened to the wind. Suddenly he knew exactly what his dad would say to him.

"Winston, didn't we teach you all the rules you would ever need? The seven rules? You broke Rules One and Two. You got hurt. You've got to live with that. But that doesn't mean you can't follow the rest. Like Rule Three: Take care of your family. You can do that."

The sensation of knowing what his dad would have said was so powerful, almost palatable, Cutter would later remember it as actually hearing his dad's voice. He knew it wasn't real but it felt so true. He listened to his dad's advice. Made up his mind to move back home and take care of Livingston and Jordan, the best he could. Worry about fixing the Sandy/Cutter problem later. But take care of his family. Treat other people how he wanted to be treated. And dammit, have fun.

The Williams Thanksgiving was as loud and chaotic and warm as always. It was just the tonic Cutter needed. After dinner some of the nephews got a poker game up and Cutter joined in, listening to the constant ribbing and joshing between the cousins and feeling better than he had in three and a half months. He lost lots of dollar bills, especially on the hand he threw in so the youngest at the table, seven year old Carson, could finally win a hand. He gorged himself on three slices of pumpkin pie, until he thought he might throw up. Only when the family gathered and had a Thanksgiving prayer did Cutter suddenly miss his kids and feel sad. He changed his ticket and flew home the next morning on the first flight out.

At about the time Cutter was losing the big bucks at poker, the Carrolls and their guests, the Richards, were finishing a very formal Thanksgiving dinner. Ty suggested to Cord they have a drink in the study. "So where do we stand with Riverside?" Ty asked as soon as Cord closed the door.

"Seems to me we are in great shape," Cord replied. "Lois and her board up at the Jake loved the new design, especially when I told them it would cost them nothing extra. All the demolition work has been done, and all the underground utilities laid. We'll be moving some dirt and digging some basements during the winter and as soon as the thaw occurs, building construction will start." Cord was very pleased with the progress.

Ty nodded and then his face darkened. "What about this thing you apparently have with Sandy Williams? Looks to me like your wife is more than a little bit bent out of shape with you. This isn't going to blow up, is it? Don't make me remind you we need the Williams guy around 'til after the Jake?"

Now Cord's face changed color, only his color was red. He couldn't help himself, he stammered. "No. No.

Everything is fine, boss. I've got everything under control. You have nothing to worry about," he told him, though he was more than a little nervous. Sandy had told him about Cutter leaving for Thanksgiving, and she was worried he might do something stupid, like not coming back. And then she warned Cord that things couldn't stay as they were, and he might have to make up his mind.

"Good," Ty said. "Just make sure you keep it that way."

Sandy was not having a good holiday. In order to make things seem normal for Jordan, she had cooked a small turkey and other traditional items for the three of them but found she could not eat. After dinner she cleaned up and threw out all the leftovers and watched a Christmas cartoon movie with Jordan. Put the kids to bed and drank a whole bottle of wine by herself.

At ten o'clock the next morning, Cutter walked in the front door and sat his suitcase at the foot of the stairs. Jordan and Livingston ran up to him, each grabbing a leg. Even the damned dog seemed happy to see him. Sandy stood on the other side of the room, arms folded. "Hey, guys," Cutter said, getting down on his knees and hugging them together.

"Are you coming home?" Jordan asked, her voice trembling.

"You bet, Shortcakes. I couldn't leave you guys for very long."

She hugged him around the neck and whispered in his ear, "I knew you weren't an asshole, Daddy."

Sandy turned and walked out of the room without saying a word, but as soon as her back was to Cutter, she smiled.

SEVENTEEN

Cutter had moved back in, but only with his kids, not his wife. He moved his stuff into the guest bedroom. Jordan noted it but said nothing. She didn't want him to change his mind and move back out. And she found there was the additional benefit of him letting her stay when she crawled into his bed in the middle of the night. He even let her bring Baily with her. He also seemed like everything was okay. He joked with her like he used to do, kidding around. He was making breakfast for them and reading them stories at night. She had discovered during his absence the stories as he read them were not the stories her mother read to them. His didn't always say the same things and he was lots sillier. But she didn't correct him She didn't know the word *jinx*, but she sure didn't want to do that now that her life was back in order.

Cutter was lots happier. He noticed, too, Sandy seemed to get more irritated the happier he acted. Never one to pass up an opportunity to be passive aggressive, Cutter laughed and giggled and talked with the kids constantly. He smiled all the time. Even made nice with Baily. He whistled Christmas songs. Found he really did feel better when he acted like he felt better. Work was enjoyable now. The department budget had passed as requested, so he was able to buy new equipment, give some raises, and let staff try some new programs. He knew it would just be a temporary increase in morale, but it came at a perfect time.

The holidays flew by. Sandy didn't want to go to Iowa, which was fine with Cutter. She did want to go to the Richards' New Year's Eve party, but Cutter refused and told her to go by herself. She wouldn't and they passed the evening in separate rooms. Cutter wasn't sure what was going on with Sandy and Cord. She seemed to spend more time at home. When he first came back, he had to work at resisting the temptation to spy on her, but now he found he didn't even want to know what she was doing.

After the first of the year, Cutter had more time on his hands and once again started thinking about the Riverside Park recording, as he referred to it. He did some research, or more correctly, he had Rachel actually do the research on how to track real estate sales, and the two of them spent a couple of weeks, off and on, in the Chaffee County courthouse reviewing real estate deals over the last couple of years. They could find no trend nor any single individual or company which was purchasing property around Riverside Park.

In late March, the final construction plans for the Jacob Matthew Cup facilities reached his desk for approval. Cutter couldn't help but be impressed. He ran them by the mayor and the new president of city council, as well as his boss, Hugh Stalter. All of them were equally impressed and asked Cutter how much could be saved after the event was over—as a historical-cultural-entertainment attraction, which incidentally might become a big money-making proposition for the city. Cutter told them he didn't see much value in keeping the dorms, since they had been designed as apartments, not hotel rooms, but agreed the city should consider keeping the rest as a tourist attraction.

Finally, before he actually signed off on them, Cutter took the plans to show Bart Jones. Black Bart looked them over carefully and announced he could see no reason why Cutter shouldn't sign off on them. Cutter then told him about their extended search of property transactions and their failure to turn up anything which looked like a real estate conspiracy.

"Yeah, I don't know," Jones said. "It's all very strange. I do have a couple of other ideas I'm gonna check out next time I'm in Denver. You know, the kind of things which would require an expert in constitutional law. Like me, for instance."

"Terrific," Cutter told him, "I'll sleep more peacefully at night having such a learned legal scholar covering my backside."

"For an exorbitant fee, naturally," Jones countered.

"Naturally."

Within days after the plans were approved, a ten foot high fence was installed to block off the construction site. Then the equipment and materials started streaming into the park. Cutter was amazed to see the speed at which things were being done. The two ice arenas were started first and the groundbreaking for the performance hall quickly followed. He was fascinated by it all.

The approval of the plans also meant Cutter and Sandy had no business to discuss. They talked only about the kids, but otherwise they lived solitary lives together. To Cutter marriage felt like a distant memory, something he had done once in his life, a long time ago. Lord only knew what Sandy was thinking. She had never been much of one to share her feelings. In Cutter's head if this thing of theirs was to be fixed, it was up to Sandy to make the first move. So far she had shown not a bit of interest in making any moves.

Cutter's second anniversary with the department came and went. It was now mid-June and the slower pace of a park director's work life was in full swing. Cutter spent his days visiting parks and employees, checking the progress of the Jake construction, playing golf and taking naps on the couch in his office. He had just fallen asleep one perfect midafternoon when he was awakened by Rachel.

"Cutter, wake up," she said softly.

Cutter rubbed his eyes and sat up. He started to speak and Rachel held her finger to her lips, signaling for him to stay quiet. She stepped back and kicked her shoes off gently. She then reached behind her back and slowly unzipped her dress and let it slide to the floor. Cutter heard himself gasp. She had nothing on underneath. And Cutter had never seen such a perfect body. Every muscle was perfectly toned and her flawless skin was an electric tan. Her straight glossy pitch black hair hung almost to her waist, though Cutter couldn't figure out where she kept all that hair when she was dressed. She had perfect breasts, right down to her perfect nipples. A flat stomach that ended in a perfect triangle of soft black hair. She put her finger to her lips again and walked over to Cutter, took his hands and helped him stand in front of her. Starting at the top, she slowly unbuttoned his shirt and then put her hands on his stomach and ran them up his chest to his shoulders so the shirt slid down his arms and dropped off his back. She edged back a small step and undid his belt and jeans button and very slowly slid down the zipper, slowly enough that he could swear he heard each click. She put her fingers inside the waistband of the boxers and pushed down just hard enough that boxers and jeans fell to the floor around his ankles. And said, louder this time, "C'mon, Cutter, wake up. Your attorney is here and says he has to speak with you right now."

Cutter blinked his eyes awake and sat up quickly. Christ in a handbasket. I better figure out a way to get laid soon, or I'm going to get myself into real trouble.

"What?" he asked.

"Your attorney is here. Jones. Obnoxious. But he says he has to see you right now."

"Okay. Tell him I'll be out in a minute," Cutter told her, trying to cover for the fact that he couldn't stand right now without giving away the bulging clue to his teenage fantasy. Rachel gave him a look like he had just dropped in from another planet, started to say something and changed her mind, whirled and left his office. Five minutes later, Cutter had composed himself and went to collect Black Bart from the lobby.

195

"Attorney Jones, so nice to have you visit."

Bart looked at him and shook his head. "You may want to reconsider that statement in a few minutes," Bart told him and, without asking, led the way back to Cutter's office.

"What exciting news are you bringing me?" Cutter asked Bart's back.

After they were seated on Cutter's couch, the lawyerly Bart said, "Cutter, do you remember what I told you the night I suggested you hire me?"

"Something about my needing a lawyer to protect my ass."

"More importantly, I told you public employees always fuck up. I had started to believe you might be the exception. I should have realized as a constitutional lawyer I am never wrong."

"What did I fuck up?"

Bart handed him a copy of an old Denver newspaper article which looked to Cutter to be very ancient, maybe a hundred years old or older. He looked for the year it was written and there was none. He read the short article.

> Columbus
>
> Tuesday, May 5
>
> Today, the esteemed Christopher Carroll, our illustrious founder, further demonstrated his unwavering dedication to the citizens of Columbus, Colorado by donating a large tract of land to be used for a public park. The land borders

the Arkansas River and is the site where the original town was founded. As part of his magnanimous donation, Mr. Carroll has burned down all the derelict buildings on the site and caused all of the debris remaining to be removed. Mr. Carroll has deeded the property to the City Government and the deed was happily accepted, amid many speeches and well wishes, by the mayor, the Right Honorable Justin Callaham, and members of the City Council. When by proclamation the council deemed the new park to be named Carroll Park, Mr. Carroll declined the honor and asked that the park instead be named Riverside Park. Mr. Carroll will also make available funds for numerous improvements to the new park and told those gathered it is his wish Riverside Park become as grand as the Central Park of New York City. He also wished to insure all future generations of Columbus residents would always be guaranteed the usage of the park in that he included in the deed transfer the requirement that no future city officials should have the right to sell, transfer, donate or close for more than twenty four months the property or the city would forfeit the park and it would be

returned to the heirs of Mr. Carroll. Mr.
Carroll was given a five minute standing
ovation by those in attendance.

The article went on to name all those in attendance
and to describe, in great detail, what all the women present were wearing.

Cutter finished reading and looked up at Bart. "I don't
get it. What does this mean? How did I fuck up?"

"You, a city official, have closed the park for
more than two years. If a copy of the deed can be
found, the Carroll heirs would have a claim on the
property."

"But one, no one seems to have a copy of the deed;
and two, it's not really closed and is still going to be a
public park. Oh, and three, Ty Carroll is helping make
the improvements in the park." Cutter paused.

Black Bart smiled and said, "Wait for it, wait for it..."
Thirty seconds later, Cutter looked as if someone had hit
him in the face with a brick. Bart added, "And there it is."

Cutter, eyes wide, said quietly, "You're telling me if Ty
or his family, or anyone for that matter, has a copy of
the deed, the Carroll family could take the park for their
personal use?"

"For a dumb public servant, you catch on pretty quick.
That's exactly what it means. And not just the land, but
every building, every appurtenance, every improvement.
Which of course would include the very nice little
downtown area now being created. Along with all those
nice new apartments being built for the athletes. And still

have over 500 acres more to develop, with new infrastructure already in place. If a copy of the deed exists."

Cutter brightened. "Oh, yeah. Nobody has been able to find a copy. Maybe we're just being paranoid."

"Geez, Cutter, I thought you were figuring things out. You know Ty. What do you think the chances are they don't have a copy? Does it strike you as the kind of thing that family would let slide? My bet would be they have a copy of every deed ever filed in this county."

Cutter's shoulders collapsed, he bent over and put his head in his hands. He sat that way for several minutes, not speaking. Finally, "Well, Mr. Constitutional Lawyer, what do we do?"

"What you mean 'we', Kemo Sabe?" Bart grinned.

"Come on, Bart, I'm serious. What do you think I should do?"

"Pray. Get on your horse and ride for the hills. Prepare to be the second most hated man in Columbus. If Ty takes the park back." Jones turned serious. "Maybe you should just go ask Ty Carroll what his intentions are. Maybe we are just being paranoid. But at least you'll get an idea of the lay of the land."

Cutter got up and paced around the room. Stopped at the window and looked out for a while. Turned back around and told Bart, "I suppose you're right. That's where I'll start. Do I face any legal liability? Can I be sued?"

"I don't think so, but anyone can sue anyone. For any reason."

They chatted for a while longer and Bartholomew Jones took his leave. Cutter sat at his desk for an hour, reviewing all he had heard. Thought about Mayor Humphrey talking to someone about closing the park. He came to the realization his own desire to be a hero and to do something for which he would be remembered had gotten him into this mess, but for the life of him, he couldn't figure out how he had been so manipulated. How had he found out about the Jake? Why did he want to bid on it? Why did he think of Riverside as the perfect place? He knew those were all his ideas.

Sandy. Of course. Sandy. She had brought him the article and suggested bidding on it. But he had come up with Riverside. She never mentioned it. All she had ever said was why not use parkland. Wait. She said that within days of his talking about all the improvements Riverside needed. That bitch. She knew I would jump at it and then think I had come up with the Riverside idea. But what does she get out of this? Does she know about the deed restriction, the reversion clause?

He ran out of his office and went straight to Sandy's office. She was not in. He went home and waited for her. He met her at the door, drinks in hand, bourbon for her and an airplane gin and tonic for himself. She was surprised. She took the drink and sipped a little. Followed Cutter into the kitchen.

"What's going on? Where are the kids? What's with you fixing me a drink?"

"We need to talk," he told her.

She tensed, sensing the worst, and stammered quickly, "It's over with Cord. You and I can work this out."

"Fuck, I don't give a shit about that. What I do want to know is why you wanted to use Riverside Park for an event you wanted to bring here," he barked at her, though, in truth, her saying the affair was over thrilled him.

"What?"

"You heard me. Why did you push me to use Riverside for an event? Did you come up with that on your own, or did Ty Carroll or Cord have you do it?" Cutter couldn't keep the anger out of his voice.

Now Sandy looked shocked. She started to respond and stopped. Finally she asked him quietly, "How did you find out about that?"

"It doesn't matter how I found out. What did they tell you?"

"Cord told me about the opportunity and suggested I talk you into bidding on the Jake. He also said it would really be great if we used Riverside because it had fallen on hard times, and he knew his boss really wanted to see it restored. He talked Ty into putting up money and helping with it."

"Did they tell you why?"

She looked at him sternly and said, "I just told you why. Because Cord said Ty would like to see it restored to its former grandeur."

Cutter thought for a few minutes and then said to his wife, "Finish your drink so we can go get the kids."

"That's it?"

"That's it for now," he answered and drained the last of his gin and tonic.

The next morning, Cutter was sitting in the lobby when Ty Carroll entered his office. Ty smiled when he saw Cutter and walked over, his hand out. "Good morning, Director. To what do I owe the honor of your visit?"

Cutter ignored the hand and stood. "Can we talk for a few minutes?"

"Why, certainly. Would you like some coffee?"

"No. Just a couple minutes of your time." Cutter followed Carroll into his office and declined the offer of a chair. "I'll stand. This won't take long."

The smile left Ty's face. Steel in his voice, "What is it?"

"Do you have a copy of the deed to Riverside Park?"

Now Ty smiled his mountain lion smile. "Why, no. Why would I? Whatever are you talking about?"

"I think you know exactly what I'm talking about. Your plan to steal the park from the citizens of Columbus."

Ty continued to smile and shook his head. "My dear boy. We would do nothing to harm the fine citizens of this city. You must be delusional. And even if you aren't, you need to consider everything that has happened. YOU came up with the idea of hosting the Jacob Matthew Cup, YOU came up with the idea of using Riverside Park, YOU have signed all the documents as the legal guardian of the property. Anything goes wrong with the citizens' interests in the property, it falls squarely on YOU."

Cutter glared at him.

"Is there anything else I can do for you this fine morning? No? Well, then I'm sure you need to be on your way." With that, Ty took Cutter's arm and led him to the door. "Have a great day," he said to Cutter's back.

Christ in a handbasket. It must be time for a beer.

EIGHTEEN

Cutter spent several days trying to figure out how he might keep Riverside Park out of the clutches of the Carroll family and its horde of evil henchmen. He could, in fact, understand Ty and his desire for even more money and power. It seemed to come naturally to those who inherited wealth. They acted as if it were their God-given right to have so much more than others. What really, really pissed him off was Cord Richards. He had acted the part of a good, a very good friend, just to increase his own wealth and power. Cutter had trusted him. Valued him. Fucking whore. He wondered if Cord had always been that way. If any of the stories about his past had been true. Decided it didn't make any difference. Cutter knew he had been played. Time to get in the game and play back. But how?

Cutter walked into Rachel's office and closed the door. She looked up at him from her spread sheets and asked, "What can I do for you, Director?"

"Rach, I've screwed up. I've screwed you, the rest of the employees and, for that matter, every citizen of the city." She started to get up from her desk, and he waved her back down. "I need your help. You are the smartest person here—hell, you should have been director instead of me—and maybe you can help with a problem I can't fix. A problem so big you won't believe it."

By the time she heard all this, the normally imperturbable Rachel was visibly piqued. "Cutter, what the hell are you talking about?"

He told her the whole story, including the part about Sandy and Cord having an affair. When he got to that part of the story she told him, "Gee, Cutter, I am so sorry. The chief and I have our problems but nothing that terrible."

He finished with, "So there it is. I think I have cost the city its most important asset. I've traded the family cow for a handful of useless magic beans."

Rachel smiled at him. She really, really liked this guy. He was the best boss she had ever had. He was funny and genuine and seemed to care about her and the other employees. She felt bad he was in this mess. "Cutter, have you told Hugh and the mayor yet? I think that's where you should start. We don't really know how this will end. The park hasn't been closed for twenty-four months yet, so there is still time."

Cutter just looked at her. Of course, the park hasn't been closed for twenty-four months yet. Just figure out how to get it open before the deadline. Without violating our contract with the Jake and being sued for everything I've got. Rachel is right. Start with Hugh and Ham and Eggs. Cutter grinned and told her, "See, that's why you should be the director. You're the smart one." He bobbed his head up and down and walked out.

205

As soon as he was back at his desk, he called the mayor and Hugh, inviting them to join him for a beer after work. They both agreed to meet him at the Aspen Ridge Brewery. He still had no idea how he could fix this, but it felt good to be doing something, anything.

By the time the three were finishing their second beer, Cutter had told them everything he knew. Both thought about what he had said. Finally, Ham and Eggs shook his head and told them, "I don't know. That sure doesn't sound like Ty Carroll to me. He has always acted like he really cares about the city. I don't think he would do something like steal a park from the people."

Hugh looked surprised. "You've got to be kidding, Mr. Mayor. This is exactly the kind of thing he would do. Maybe because you have been on the inside, one of Ty's chosen, if you will, you don't see it. But Ty Carroll would sell his own mother into slavery for more money or more power. Yeah, I think Cutter is right. Ty Carroll is going to take the park." The enormity of what he had just said seemed to settle in Hugh's face. He now looked stricken. He finally turned to Cutter, questions on his face.

Cutter told him, told both of them, "Look, this is my screw up. I'm going to fall on the sword and resign, but I don't want to do that until we see if we can come up with a way to keep Riverside. I sure don't want to turn tail and run and leave you guys holding the bag."

The mayor said, "Oh, I'm sure we'll have plenty of time to blame you if such a thing would happen, but let's not get ahead of ourselves. I think I should just go talk to Ty and see what he has to say. Ask for his assurance the park will remain public."

"And if he gives you that assurance? What? You take his word?" Hugh sounded skeptical.

The mayor stared at him. Cutter interrupted, "You know, gentlemen, I feel as if I have been played from the moment I stepped foot in Columbus. I think Ty Carroll would tell you the same thing he told me. And I personally believe it would be a lie."

"So what do we do, Director?" Ham and Eggs asked.

"As my CFO, Rachel Red Cloud, so ably pointed out to me, the park has not yet been closed for twenty four months. We have time. Do you guys know Bartholomew Jones?"

Hugh snickered. "Yeah, I know that mongrel weasel. He cost the university a bundle of money several years ago. An older alum was going to donate a lot of land to us, but his heirs had him declared incompetent and sent Jones as their representative. He managed to get the university to buy the land and pay more than it was actually worth by convincing the president he would embarrass the whole university by saying the president knew the old man was senile and was taking advantage of him. The president folded faster than an old lady holding a seven-high poker hand." Hugh actually smiled at the memory. Then asked Cutter, "Why do you ask?"

Cutter reddened. "Uh, he's my attorney. He's the one who found the article. I think we should talk to him."

The mayor harrumphed, "Don't think so, Son, don't think so. We should talk to the city attorney. He's our legal rep."

Hugh shook his head violently and told the mayor, "No. I think Cutter is correct. Since we have absolutely no proof the Carrolls will do anything, the city attorney can't help us. Also, why would he want to shoot accusations toward his chief campaign funder?" He turned to Cutter. "Call Jones. See if he'll meet with us. Off the record."

"Yes sir," Cutter told him and waved at the waiter for the check.

The next morning they were in Jones' office where the attorney ran through his constitutional lawyer litany, ending with "Of course, my services will cost you a lot."

Hugh told him, "Bill Cutter," without a note of sarcasm in his voice.

Black Bart, equally as serious, responded, "Blood from a stone."

"Very funny," Cutter said, then told Jones about his conversations with Sandy, Ty, Hugh and the mayor. He ended with, "We want to know what, if any, legal actions we can take to block any attempt to land grab the park. You know, from a constitutional standpoint."

Bart got up and paced around the room. Stared out his window for a couple of minutes. At last, he returned to his desk and sat down, folding his hands in front of him. And, in his professorial voice lectured them, "You can't just pull the plug on the Jake. You not only incur the financial liability of the Jake having to relocate, which would be incredibly expensive, you also leave yourselves and the city open to huge lawsuits, including from Ty himself, since he is the primary guarantor of the event locally."

He continued, "What you need is a way to force Ty into signing an agreement that he and his family will never lay claim to Riverside Park, you know, on the outside chance such an opportunity would ever present itself to them. The only way I know to get his signature would be to make it, say, financially unreasonable for him not to. Does that make sense?"

Hugh shook his head. "But how would we do that?"

Jones continued, "Well, I wouldn't know anything about that kind of thing, but you could, I suppose, make it appear his investment in this whole deal is at risk."

Hugh shook his head again. "I don't get it. How the hell could we do that?" He was getting pissed at Jones. "Cutter, do you have any idea what the fuck he means? Pardon my French."

Cutter was as clearly in the dark as his boss. But Ham and Eggs' head was bobbing up and down, and he was smiling.

"Glad to see one of you isn't so dense," Bart said and asked the mayor, "What do you think?"

"Seems to me, Mr. Jones, seems to me, if some outside entity could threaten a real construction slow down or shut down, the folks up at the Jacob Mathew Cup offices might get upset enough to threaten to take Ty's money. Like you said, he is the one who guaranteed funding."

Jones slowly shook his head but had trouble keeping a straight face. "Well, now, I don't know anything about such things, but you might have a point. My legal advice to you all as city officials, is whatever happens, you have NOTHING to do with it."

By this time, Hugh and Cutter were completely lost, but both were glued to the conversation. Ham and Eggs asked Bart, "Now, Jones, if someone did have a beef with this whole thing and wanted to take action, would you represent them?"

"For a huge fee, of course," Jones replied.

The mayor smiled and said, "But of course. Billed to Director Williams, you understand."

"Of course. It goes without saying."

Cutter could no longer stand it. He jumped in, "Okay, you two, enough. Tell us what we have to do."

Bartholomew Jones stood and held up his hands. "Excuse me, but I think it's time I take my leave and let you men discuss…well, whatever it is you might want to discuss. I'm sure it is something I need not know about."

Before he left, he took a handful of his business cards and wrote a small *CW* in the corner of each and handed them to the mayor. "You might want to pass these along to anyone you think may need to talk to me or need my services. Or to anyone who might wish me to speak with Mr. Carroll."

"What's the *CW* for?" the mayor asked.

"So I know to bill Cutter Williams," Black Bart grinned. "Well, I'm sure I have another client with a constitutional emergency I must attend to. Good luck, gentlemen." And he was gone.

As soon as the door closed behind the attorney, Hugh barked at the mayor, "So what are you guys talking about? What are we going to do?"

"Before I answer that," Ham and Eggs told him, "We're going to need a few thousand dollars for, uh, er, expenses. Can you get that?"

"I could call Geren Randolph. I'm sure he would help, especially if it is something that will stick in Ty Carroll's craw."

"Call him."

"Now?"

"Now."

Hugh placed the call and got Geren to agree to front some funds, no questions asked. As soon as he hung up, he turned to the mayor and demanded, "Time to tell us what you have in mind."

The Right Honorable Mayor Hammond Eggleston laid out his plan. "Sometime next week several community groups are going to stage a series of demonstrations at the construction entrances to Riverside Park. They will carry signs and placards that demand the park be reopened and construction stopped unless their demands are met. Their demands will only be presented, in private, to Ty Carroll by the legal representative of those groups, one Bartholomew Jones. Their single demand will be that Mr. Carroll sign an agreement which will

211

renounce any current or future claims the Carroll family might have on Riverside Park and to affirm the park will belong to the citizens of Columbus in perpetuity."

Cutter finally found his voice, "And if Ty refuses?"

The mayor smiled. "I would guess the demonstrations might escalate. But that's only a guess."

Hugh asked, "Why would any group demonstrate? Risk arrest. I don't get it."

Again the mayor smiled. "You know, Hugh, I didn't spend years helping community groups without making a few friends and collecting a few chits. Good time to spend them. Good time."

Hugh pondered for a few minutes, rubbing his bald head and for the first time smiled. "You know, Mr. Mayor, you're not just another pretty face. What can we do to help?"

"I think you do what you guys would do if you knew nothing about it. For instance, Cutter will probably have to call the police to break up the demonstrations. Maybe meet with the demonstrators. See what happens. See what happens."

They shook hands and left, each to his life. Cutter was greatly relieved, though still not sure the mayor's plan, or Bart's more likely, would work. But with the pressure of this problem ebbing, Sandy crept back into his mind. What did she really know and when did she really know it and what was her part in all this? He decided to take a wait-and-see approach.

Ten days later, construction crews arrived at work early in the morning to find all five construction entrances to Riverside Park blocked by large groups of people. They carried signs which read "Open Our Park," "Save Riverside" and "Kill the Jake." They marched back and forth in front of the gates and allowed no equipment or people to enter. Within minutes, news vans and trucks showed up, just in time to go live for the 7:00 a.m. broadcasts.

At 7:02 both Cutter's and Sandy's cell phones rang. The construction manager wanted Sandy to tell him what to do. Cutter's call came from the project engineer who wanted Cutter to call the police to "get these ass-holes the hell away from my site." By the 7:30 broadcast, three of the spokespersons had given interviews at three different gates. All three interviews sounded oddly alike, almost rehearsed. Each one said they wanted the park reopened and referred all other questions to their attorney, Bartholomew Jones. At 7:40 the police arrived and tried, with not much success, to convince the demonstrators to leave peacefully. Just in time for the 8:00 live broadcast, the police started dragging demonstrators away from the gates, arresting a few. By 11:00 a.m. Bart Jones had bailed eight demonstrators out of jail.

Also at 11:00 Ty Carroll scowled at the two people standing in front of his desk, Cord Richards and Sandy Williams. In the quietest of voices, he asked them, "Would you two mind telling me what the fuck is going on? Have you lost control? How did you not see this coming? And what are you going to do to stop this silliness?"

"Boss," Cord began, "we have absolutely no idea what this is about. We heard no demands beforehand. And worse, other than 'We want our park open', we have heard nothing else. We were referred to an attorney named Jones, who so far has not returned our calls."

"What can you add?" he glared at Sandy.

"Nothing, sir. I only know what you and Cord know."

"What does your husband say?"

"I haven't talked to him about it."

"Goddammit, woman, what am I paying you for? Ask him. I have a suspicion he might know."

"Yes sir."

When she asked Cutter, he just shrugged his shoulders and said nothing.

Three weeks later, the media had lost interest, but the demonstrations had continued and the arrests continued and construction fell further and further behind. Sandy flew to Denver to assure the Jake folks that they would take care of this problem and would be finished with construction with time to spare. Bartholomew Jones, Constitutional Lawyer, called Ty Carroll's office and asked for an appointment.

The next day Ty, Cord and Sandy received Bart in Ty's office. Bart told Ty he would only talk to Ty alone. Ty frowned but sent his two folks out and then demanded, "What do you guys want?"

Jones smiled and retrieved a one page document from his briefcase and slid it across the desk. "Sign this and all your problems disappear. Well, at least the problems with Riverside Park disappear."

Ty read the page, his black eyes turning even darker and the tendons in his neck tightening. He did not look up. He read it a second time. He methodically tore the document into little pieces and dropped them into a wastebasket under his desk. "Mr. Jones, fuck you. And fuck all those assholes who think they can boss me around. I own this town. Remember that. Now get the hell out of my office."

Bartholomew Jones rose, picked up his briefcase and walked out, winking at Cord and Sandy as he passed them in the ante room.

NINETEEN

The following morning construction crews and their police escorts showed up at the entrance gates to Riverside Park where, to their surprise, not one picketer showed his face. Within the hour, Ty Carroll got the news and could not help smiling. He was somewhat amazed his handling of the demonstrators' attorney had such a quick impact, and gave the guy credit for being smart enough to figure out who he was up against. He walked over to Cord's office just to make sure his assistant understood how one really used power to get things done.

When quitting time for the construction crews rolled around, they packed up their tools and secured their equipment and headed to their vehicles to go home. For the first time in several weeks they had actually gotten in a whole day's work, thanks to being able to get onto the site on time. Not one of the workers knew what had happened, but they were all glad not to have to sit around until the gates were opened for them. Then they got to the gates to leave. Which were blocked by more demonstrators than they had ever seen in the mornings. Hundreds of people. With no police around to help them get out.

Construction workers who are kept away from their work are irritated. Construction workers who are kept from their post-work shots and beers, softball or pool games, girlfriends and boyfriends and mates, or pizza and sports on TV are insanely pissed. It took only about ten minutes of confusion growing to anger for the tire irons and hammers to come out. Over the next fifteen minutes the demonstrations had turned into riots. By the time the police arrived, enough fights had broken out to send almost a dozen people to the hospital and another thirty injured but attended to on site. The news crews had arrived minutes before the police, and all the evening news shows were able to show film of bleeding heads and bodies lying on the ground.

First thing the following morning, Bart Jones sat in the waiting room at Ty Carroll's office. He didn't have an appointment but figured Ty might want to see him first thing. He was ushered into Ty's office and, without saying a word, laid another copy of the one page document on Ty's desk. Ty picked up the phone, punched one number and said, "Security? Would you please come remove a man from my office? Thank you." And hung up. Bart turned on his heel without speaking and walked out.

The following day, hundreds of protestors, many uninvited, showed up at the gates to Riverside. Instead of blocking the gates, however, they stormed onto the property. By the time the police arrived, a substantial amount of damage had been inflicted upon the facilities under construction. Dozens of people were arrested.

Damages ran into the thousands of dollars. Bart Jones spent the entire day attending arraignments and bailing folks out of jail. He called Cutter from the courthouse just to tell him he was having the most fun he had had in years. But he added the caveat that Cutter was going to pay for all of it. He told Cutter, "You know, I really do love this constitutional law work."

Ty's secretary called Cord and told him Ty wanted to see Cord and Sandy at seven the next morning. "Listen, you two, I want this fixed by tonight. Do you understand?" Ty said to them as they stood before him.

Cord told him, "I'm not sure we can fix this. We can't figure out how this all happened, but I think our plan to keep the park closed for 24 months ain't going to work. Boss, I think we have to back off and come up with another way to gain ownership of the park for you."

Sandy stared at Cord. "What do you mean, gain ownership of the park?"

Ty glared at her. "Are you a complete moron? What do you think this is all about? What? Is this just about your proving your power by getting him into your bed?" nodding toward Cord. "You must be dumber than your husband. Who, incidentally, is the dumbest white man I ever met."

Sandy's eyes grew wide and filled with tears. She looked at Ty and then at Cord. She couldn't breathe. Once a man had used her, and she vowed then for it to never ever happen again. How could she be so gullible? She turned toward Cord and started to say something to him, then stopped. Instead, she mentally measured the distance between them and lashed her foot out, catching him squarely in the balls. "Fuck you." She turned to Ty. "And fuck you." She walked out, so many tears in her eyes she could not see.

Sandy drove home, hoping Cutter would be there. He wasn't. She poured herself a bourbon, then another. When Cutter finally got home, he found Sandy sitting on the step of the front porch. Even though it was mid-August, the hottest time of the year, Sandy was shivering. She stood and walked down the steps to him, put her arms around his neck. He remained motionless. She hugged very hard, but he did not return it. "Cutter, I am so sorry. I didn't know. I swear I didn't," she said softly into his ear.

He gently lifted her arms from his shoulders and dropped them. They fell to her sides. "I always thought you were the smart one. I trusted you," he said to her.

"I'll make it up to you. I promise."

"I sincerely doubt it." He walked past her into the house.

Lois Borin, the Executive Director of the Jacob Matthew Cup, was a diminutive former figure skater. Four feet, ten inches tall, maybe ninety pounds at her heaviest. She had been a very good skater. In fact, had her partner not dropped her and broken her ankle during practice, she would have been one of America's best hopes for a gold medal at the Olympics. But her personality was anything but diminutive. One didn't get to be Executive Director by being a shrinking violet. Lois had had enough.

At the same time Ty was telling his assistants to fix the Riverside Park problem, Lois was talking with protestors at the main construction entrance. All she could get out of them was to talk to their attorney, and they gave her Bart's card.

Lois looked at the horsehead emblem on Jones' card and smirked. Great, I'm trying to fix this, and I have to talk to a would-be paladin. She drove to Jones' office and waited for him to arrive. When he did, she introduced herself and politely asked for a few minutes of his time, which he gladly gave her. Well, not gave her. He would bill Cutter.

"Mr. Jones, I was referred to you by a rather burly man carrying a huge sign which said 'Open Our Park'. He told me you are the only one who can fix this mess." Lois' countenance hardened so dramatically it gave the attorney a chill. "So fix it," she demanded.

Bart reached into a file on his desk and slid a single sheet of paper toward her. "You get Ty Carroll to sign this and all the problems stop. But not until he signs this."

Lois read the document and looked up. "I don't get this. What does this have to do with the Jake?"

"There is the possibility should the park be closed for more than 24 months, as it will be for the Jake, the Carroll family could lay claim to the property. By signing this document they relinquish any such claim."

Lois stood to her full four foot ten. Bart would later claim she looked to be over six feet tall. "Thank you," she said softly and left his office, document in hand.

Twenty minutes later she was in Ty's office. She waited until he came to greet her. He smiled and asked "What can I do for you today, Ms. Borin?"

She explained to him while she truly appreciated everything he had done for them in the past, this continuing bad publicity was devastating, and her board wanted her to move the event away from Columbus. Immediately. Oh, and they would regrettably have to collect on Ty's guarantees.

Ty did his best to look offended. "Isn't there any way we can fix this?"

"Sign this. Right now."

He looked at the document and swore under his breath. Mentally moved Bartholomew Jones to the top of his revenge list. Ty Carroll was smart enough to know when he was beaten. He signed the document and pushed it back to her.

"Thank you." It was the only thing she said before she walked out. Within the hour, the document was delivered to Jones and every protestor and demonstrator disappeared, as if by magic, from the Riverside Park site.

Ty sat at his desk and tried to figure out how his plan had gone so awry. Certainly Cutter Williams had had some part in it, and maybe because of his wife. Jones was just a hatchet man, albeit a good one. Cord should have been savvy enough to figure out what was going on, but apparently he had started to think with his dick, not his head. But if Sandy didn't know about the plan, and obviously she didn't before today, then how had Cutter discovered it? Who else might have known?

Humphrey. That idiot asshole. Well, all of them had to be dealt with. Couldn't have anyone believe Ty Carroll had been bested.

"Cord, come in here for a minute," Ty barked into his phone. Thirty seconds later, Cord stood in front of him.

"Yes, sir?"

"I want Sandy Williams fired. Today."

"But, boss, she's really good at what she does. I don't think she had anything to do with this."

"I don't give a rat's ass what you think. I'm sure her husband had something to do with it; and since I can't get to him immediately, we'll start with her. Fire her, have the guards stay with her until her office is empty, and then get your ass back here."

Cord walked over to Sandy's office. Her staff said she had called to tell them she was taking the day off. He called her cell phone. No answer. He called her home. She answered with a dead voice, "Hello?"

"Baby, it's me."

"You asshole. I can't believe you lied to me. Used me. What do you want?"

"Baby, I really hate to do this, but we have to let you go. I'll have your office cleaned out and your stuff sent to you, along with your final check."

Sandy stared at the phone. She tried to contain herself, but was unsuccessful. She screamed at him, "You lying fucking son of a bitch. I hate you." She went on for a minute or so before realizing he had already hung up. She went to the kitchen window and watched Cutter playing with Jordan and Livingston in the back yard.

She poured another drink, drank it in one swallow, sat down hard on the wood floor and burst into tears. She cried until she fell asleep, curled up in a fetal ball, where Cutter found her an hour later, Baily the dog curled up beside her. He picked her up and carried her to her bed, then took the children out for pizza.

After he had overseen the removal of Sandy's belongings from her office, Cord returned to Ty's office and reported what had happened. Ty remained expressionless throughout the explanation. Cord asked, "Now what? You want me to hire a new director?"

Ty got up and walked around his desk, put his hand on Cord's shoulder and squeezed, a little too hard. "Cord, you're fired. I trusted you with the most important job our family has had for years and you blew it. Get out."

Cord knew better than to speak. He turned, went to the door of Ty's office where he was met by two very large security guards who escorted him and two boxes of his stuff to the curb. After he had handed over the keys to the leased Mercedes the company had provided him. He took a taxi home and told Beth he had been fired. All she said was, "However are we going to pay for all this?" sweeping her hand around the house. He decided he needed a drink and walked down the street to the local tavern. By the time he returned home hours later, Beth, Sabrina, Theano, all of the luggage and the family car were gone.

At eight o'clock in the evening, Ty still sat at his desk. When the last of his underlings left, he closed his door and took out a laptop computer. He opened it and went to an email account set up under a fictitious name. He wrote:

To: Chief Brian Cheffer
Columbus Police Department
From: A Concerned Citizen
Re: Murder

Chief,

About three years ago, a young woman who worked for Mayor Carleton Humphrey died in a vehicular incident which was ruled an accident. It wasn't. She was murdered. I suggest you interview the former mayor's brother, Viceroy Humphrey, also known as Horse, WITHOUT any warning to either him or the former mayor. I am sure you will find a thorough investigation will reveal the true story. I will be watching the news to make sure you do your duty.

The next morning Chief Cheffer read the email and thought, "Son of a bitch. That peckerwood Humphrey is still causing me headaches." But he called the detective he relied on for touchy jobs, Ken Dunn. "Hey, Dunn, I'm forwarding you an 'eyes only' email. You'll know what to do. Call me before you take any official action." He forwarded the email to Dunn.

That afternoon, Detective First Class Kenneth Dunn walked into the apartment Viceroy Humphrey was cleaning as an employee of the real estate company his brother worked for. Dunn flipped his long blond hair out of his eyes and held his badge out for Humphrey to see. "Horse, you're going to have to come downtown to answer a few questions."

Horse Humphrey looked stricken. He stammered, "I have to call my brother first."

"Uh uh, Horse. You can either come along now, or I'll have to arrest you and then you can make your one call. It's just a few questions." Dunn put on his I'm-your-friend-here-to-help-you face.

Horse continued to stammer, "But, but, but. I don't think I should. My brother is mayor. No, wait. He was mayor. He was your boss. I think I should talk to him first."

"Your choice. Turn around and put your hands behind you."

"No, no. I'll go. If it's just a few questions. I can do that."

Half an hour later, Dunn and Horse were in an interview room at police headquarters. Dunn had gotten Horse a Dr. Pepper and a package of Little Debbie cupcakes. Horse gobbled the cupcakes and washed them down with the soda. Dunn asked, "So, Horse, what can you tell me about a girl who worked for your brother who died in a car accident?"

Bells and sirens and flashing lights and whistles went off in Horse's head. He couldn't catch his breath. What had Carleton told him to say? A bead of sweat formed on his head. Again, he stammered " Wh-wh-what?"

Dunn repeated his question. It gave time for Horse to think, or what passed for thinking by Horse. Now he remembered exactly what he was supposed to say. "I don't know nothin' 'bout that." He grinned. He was so pleased he had remembered.

"C'mon, Horse, you can tell me. Your brother already told us everything. We just need you to verify what he told us."

"Oh, thank God," Horse thought. His brother had already taken care of this. He relaxed and smiled. "Can I have some more cupcakes?" he asked Dunn.

"Of course you can," Dunn replied and got Horse two more packages. After Horse finished those, Dunn prodded him, "Okay, so tell us your side."

Horse told him everything, about chasing the girl to get the recorder, about how he had gotten real close to her car and about how she had gone over the edge. He explained he had tried to climb down to save her, but since she was dead, he left her there after taking her recorder. Dunn asked if he had told his brother.

"Well, sure I did. He slapped me on the head and yelled at me. Then he said I should not never talk about it," Horse grinned. "And I never did." He was so happy he thought he would burst. "You make sure you tell my brother how good I did."

Dunn got Horse some more cupcakes and called Chief Cheffer, told him about the interview, listened while Cheffer told him what to do. Dunn returned to the interview room, read Horse his rights and placed him under arrest. Horse was charged with manslaughter and leaving the scene of a fatal accident. He would spend a long time in jail. With a great amount of satisfaction, Ken Dunn drove to Carleton's office and placed him under arrest for the same charges, plus concealing a felony and aiding and abetting a felon. Dunn truly hoped this asshole would do a lot of time as well.

The chief called the sheriff's office and together they announced the arrests. Jean Smith's mother saw the news and went into a whole new round of wailing. Suzie spent the next few weeks worrying the insurance company would come to try to get back what they paid on the life insurance policy. Not one person gave a bit of credence to Carleton's story that it was all done for Ty Carroll. Except Ruth Roberts, who drove south of the city and, after smashing it with a rock, threw the recorder into the Arkansas River. She then sent out resumes to a number of newspapers on the East Coast.

TWENTY

A couple of weeks after the demonstrators had disappeared as mysteriously as they had appeared, Rachel Red Cloud walked into Cutter's office and closed the door behind her. She sat down on his couch and said, "Okay, Director, tell." Cutter raised his eyebrows. "You know what I mean. I want to know how you did it."

"Did what?"

"Fixed our problem."

"I didn't do anything." She started to speak and he held up his hand to stop her. "I will tell you this. When the time comes you need some help, turn to Hugh Stalter and Hammond Eggleston."

"Why would I need to do that?"

Cutter smiled at her. "Because I think you will sit in this chair in the not too distant future, and you need to know who your friends are."

Rachel knitted her brow and frowned. "I don't want to sit in that chair. I like mine just fine when you are in that one. Tell me what happened. I assume the problem with the Carroll's claiming Riverside Park got resolved. Am I right?"

"It did. I can't tell you anymore but remember what I told you about the mayor and Hugh. Our mayor is a brilliant politician and the kind of leader that doesn't come along very often. And Hugh has balls of steel."

Their talk turned to the mundane business of running the department. When she left, Rachel felt relieved and even happier to be working for Cutter. As soon as she was gone, Cutter called Hugh, the mayor and his constitutional lawyer and asked them to dinner. His treat. It took four or five calls to get the schedules meshed, but the dinner was set for the following Monday.

After drinks had been ordered and delivered and the dinner orders taken, Cutter stood and held his beer glass high. "Gentlemen, a toast to you for what you have done for your city. Made all the more remarkable because no one will ever know what you did. And to all those folks who got arrested or their heads bashed in. The city owes them a great thank you they will never receive. And all because I screwed up so badly."

His three dinner companions had added a couple of *hear, hear*s and clinked glasses several times during his speech, but when he got to his final statement, Hugh quickly jumped in, the grin disappearing from his reddened face. "Wait just a second, Son," he corrected. "I think you have forgotten something really important. You weren't hired to turn Parks and Recreation into some kind of super agency where no mistakes are made. Hell, we didn't even care if the parks looked good or we got a bigger budget or if we had good programs. We hired you to do exactly what you did: keep the department out of the hands of Mayor Humphrey and whoever was pushing him to gain control. We now know who that was and why he wanted it. You gave us even more than we asked for. The budget is restored, the employees' morale is way up, there is a new excitement about the department and, most importantly, citizens got involved once again in standing up for their parks."

The mayor finally spoke. "True words, boy, true words. You should be proud of what you have done. We need you here. Columbus needs you. I need you."

The normally loquacious Black Bart Jones had remained unusually quiet, but he could no longer resist, "Typical political claptrap. Blah, blah, blah. But with you around, I can see me becoming a rich, very rich, man. Here." He handed Cutter a standard sized envelope with an embossed horse's head on it.

Cutter opened the envelope and took out the two sheets of paper. On top of the first page it read "Invoice for Services" below another embossed horse's head. Cutter read through the first page, trying to keep the dismay out of his expression but not succeeding. He felt a tightness in his throat as he looked through the hours and hours of billings for everything from research to court dates to preparation of briefs and interviewing arrestees. A couple hundred dollars more for office services. The number at the bottom of the page was more than half the value of his house. His very expensive, we-can't-afford-it-on-my-salary-alone-anyway house. Christ in a handbasket. He turned to the second page which was entitled "Adjustments and Mitigations." There were just two line items:

1. Deduction for the most fun I have had working on a case in my life. Followed by a figure about half the amount of the total on the first page.

2. Deduction for bringing in new clients who claim, for some unfathomable reason, they want to be represented by an attorney who bested the Carroll family. (Where they might have gotten that idea is beyond me. I told them all I am merely a simple but expensive constitutional lawyer). Followed by an amount equal to the amount under Number 1.

The final bill, after deductions, was equal to the few hundred dollars for office services.

Cutter looked up at the three faces peering intently at him. Ham and Eggs could no longer control himself. He roared with laughter and the other two joined in. Hugh had tears in his eyes and Jones shook his head and told Cutter, "You are still one of the slowest sumbitches I ever met." Cutter grinned and signaled the server for another round. They took their time eating dinner and talking, all feeling more relaxed than they had for weeks. Cutter ordered one more round of drinks after dinner.

"One final thing," Cutter told them. "Effective in six weeks, I am resigning my position." The others started to protest in unison. Cutter cut them off. "Look, I really, really appreciate your saying those nice things. But the truth is, you do need to move on. I know in my heart of hearts a lot of this mess falls on my shoulders. What was it Dirty Harry said? 'A man's got to know his limitations.' You have on staff the perfect person for the job, Rachel Red Cloud. She knows her stuff, she's savvy and the employees like and respect her. Making this change is the only reasonable thing you can do."

Hugh spoke up, "I don't care. We want you to stay."

The mayor agreed.

Cutter turned very serious. "Sorry, guys. My mind is made up. As you may know, this whole thing has been, uh, how do I say it, disruptive to my marriage. I think that might tend to make me less effective going forward."

The others all knew about Sandy's indiscretions, but all acted as if they didn't know what he was talking about. Finally, the mayor said, "We trust you to make the best decision. You just have to promise to give us two more months to make the transition."

Hugh nodded his head in agreement. "We'll talk to Rachel and see what we think. If we do have to do a search, we may need a little more time than that. Agreed?"

"Agreed. And, gentlemen," Cutter had to choke out the next words, "thank you so much for everything you have done for me."

By the time Cutter got home, he was feeling very sorry for himself. He stormed into the house, shoulders hunched almost up to his earlobes, and stomped up the stairs. Even Baily sensed his mood and hid from him. He went straight into his bedroom and closed the door. He lay on his bed and stared at the ceiling. Twenty minutes later there was a tiny little knock on the door. "Come in," he said. He sounded gruffer than he had meant to.

The door opened slowly and Livingston walked in carrying a large picture book. He laid the book on the bed next to his dad, climbed up on the bed and picked up the book. Held it out toward Cutter and asked softly, "Read me a story, Daddy?"

"Of course." Livingston flopped down at Cutter's side. Cutter looked at the still open door where Jordan stood quietly. He patted the bed next to his other side and she came in, closed the door behind her and crawled up alongside him. Finally he allowed himself a small smile. He started reading. Within five minutes, Livingston was sound asleep. He finished the story.

"Daddy, are you sad?" Jordan asked.

"Yeah, a little I guess," he told her.

"Why?"

"Stupid grownup stuff, honey. Just stupid grownup stuff."

"I'm sad too," she said quietly.

Cutter pulled her up into his lap. "Why are you sad?"

"Because Sabrina moved away, and she didn't even tell me good bye."

"I'm sorry, Shortcakes. I'm sure you'll find a new best friend. Everyone likes you." He hugged her tightly and it suddenly hit him. Wallowing in self-pity was pointless. He had this terrific kid, these terrific kids, to love.

"Will you read the story again, Daddy, but this time with the made up parts like you used to?" He smiled, hugged her again and within minutes had her laughing at his new, inane translation of the same picture book. They fell asleep soon afterwards.

At six in the morning Cutter was awakened by Livingston bouncing on his chest. "Daddy, wake up. Wake up." Cutter opened one eye, then the other. "Daddy, make me pancakes," his son commanded and bounced out of the bed. Cutter snuggled his daughter awake and they followed Livingston to the kitchen where Cutter put on coffee, poured the kids some juice and started mixing pancake batter.

Just as the pancakes were being delivered to the kids, Sandy walked into the room, rubbing her eyes. "Mommy, you want some pancakes? Daddy just made them and they're real good." Sandy looked at Cutter, a question in her eyes and he nodded yes. She sat and he poured her a cup of coffee and gave her his plate of pancakes. He started a couple more on the griddle.

Sandy spoke. "Cutter, yesterday I talked to a few of our old clients in Iowa and two of them have some work for me which I can do from here."

"That's good," he replied, "especially since I'm resigning from the city next month."

"What?" She tried to keep the anger out of her voice because the kids were there, but everyone in the room tensed.

"I'm leaving the parks department."

"What are you going to do?" her voice a little calmer.

"Find a job, I suppose. Maybe my lawyer needs a flunky around his office. Maybe I could get a job as a ski instructor." He smiled. "Or, I've got it, maybe the new parks director will hire me as a starter at the golf course. And until the course opens up, I could work on the Great American Novel."

Sandy finished her breakfast in silence, occasionally casting the *malocchio* his direction. Cutter's playful mood infected the kids, and they laughed and giggled until he hustled them upstairs to get ready for the day.

Late in the afternoon, he wandered back to Rachel's office and plopped down in the chair next to her desk. "Rachel, I'm resigning. In six weeks. I've recommended you for the director's job and Hugh says they will be talking to you soon. I'd rather you not say anything to anyone 'til I announce it."

She was all business. "Won't work," was all she said.

"Why not?"

"You've got to stay until the end of the year, at least."

"Why?"

"Because I have to do next year's budget, and I can't do both. And there's no time to train someone."

He looked at her and saw she was dead serious. He put out his hand and told her "Deal." They shook. He got up and walked toward the door.

"I really hate this, you know," she said to his back. He smiled as he left.

Over the next few weeks, the commission interviewed Rachel Red Cloud and offered her the job as director. She worked on the budget and the rest of the staff buttoned up the department for winter. Cutter tried to keep out of everyone's way. The first week of December, at his weekly staff meeting, he announced he would be leaving and his last day would be Christmas Eve. He told them the Commission had offered the job to Rachel, and she would be the new director.

His secretary, Alicia, was the first to speak. "Oh, Director, I always knew we'd get divorced someday, I just didn't expect it to be so soon." She got up, walked over and gave him a big hug.

Jerry Picker added, "You know, Harry, I hate to see you go. You're the first boss I ever had who stayed out of my way." He offered his hand to Cutter, then added, "What the hell is your name anyway?" Everyone laughed and someone asked, "Would it make a difference?" Jerry allowed as how it wouldn't.

Alan, who had hoped to be considered for the director position someday, was the first to congratulate Rachel. After the shock wore off, everyone was congratulating both Cutter and Rachel. Not one person asked why he was leaving. He was glad but a little surprised. Ah, well, people come and go so quickly around here they've probably gotten tired of asking.

The Sunday before Christmas, Ty Carroll got up from his desk and opened the wall safe behind his chair. He took out a worn leather portfolio and carefully extracted a large brown envelope which he laid on his desk. He sat down and opened the envelope, withdrawing a document well over one hundred years old. It was the last notarized copy of the deed to Riverside Park. Over the

236

course of several years, he had gotten his people into positions where they had access to the other copies, including the city attorney's office, the city clerk's office, the county recorder's office and even the state documents and records library. Every copy of the deed had been purloined and destroyed. Digital copies had been erased. But in the end it had made no difference. He had not been able to grab back the 600 acres of prime real estate.

He took out a Zippo lighter his grandfather had carried in the war. He held up the deed with two fingers and flicked the lighter to life. He held it to the corner of the deed, and the old paper caught fire quickly. As the flame started up the side of the document, he dropped the lighter and put the fire out with his hand. It burned his palm. Within those short seconds, it occurred to him while he had not been able to get the land back, maybe future generations of Carrolls would be smarter, cleverer than he. Maybe they would find a way to get back that which his great, great grandfather had so stupidly given away. He put the deed back in the envelope and the envelope back in the leather portfolio, the portfolio back in the safe. Ty Carroll smiled as he spun the tumbler to lock the safe.

Christmas Eve morning, Cutter's staff had a small combination Christmas and going-away party. Pleasantries and season's greetings were passed around like a box of inexpensive candy. At ten, as his last official act, he gave everyone the rest of the day off and stayed to answer the phones. Only Rachel remained to ask a few more director-type questions. At noon, she came to his office, coat on, to tell him goodbye. He stood and giving her his best aw-shucks grin, held out his hand. Instead of taking his hand, she gave him a very tight, very quick squeeze and whispered in his ear, "I wish we could have met at some other time, Cutter. You take care of yourself. Merry Christmas."

Cutter took her by the shoulders, held her at arm's length and said, "Me too, Rachel, me too. You have a great holiday. And call me if there is anything I can ever do for you." He turned her around and marched her, stiff armed, toward his door. She walked out and, knowing he would be watching her, she raised her hand in a salute without turning around. He waved silently to her back. Merry Christmas, Rachel Red Cloud.

In the late afternoon, Bartholomew Jones, constitutional lawyer, showed up at Cutter's office, bearing the gift of a bottle of very expensive scotch. They toasted the season and parted as if they would see each other in a few days. Cutter didn't ask him for a job.

Christmas morning, way before the sun came up, Livingston bounded into Cutter's bedroom and yelled, "Daddy, get up, get up. Santa came. Hurry." He was gone, yelling for his sister as he bounced down the stairs. Cutter rolled over and got up. This was his very favorite time of Christmas.

He went downstairs and made a pot of coffee, then back upstairs to brush his teeth and try to get his hair under control. He moved very slowly and methodically. He slowly walked back down the steps where the kids and Sandy were sitting by the Christmas tree. "Come on, Daddy. Hurry up. You do this every year. You make us wait forever," Jordan whined. It was true. He did draw things out as long as possible. It was something his father had done to him and his siblings, and he knew some day his kids would do it to his grandchildren. The tradition made him smile. He got a cup of coffee and joined them in the living room. Livingston squealed and Cutter snapped his fingers.

"Ah, shoot, I forgot to get a piece of coffee cake," he said and stood to go back to the kitchen. He asked, "Anyone else want some?"

Jordan was beside herself. "Daddy, please," she begged. He relented and sat down and Jordan passed out gifts. The festivities began. The remainder of the day was spent playing with new toys and eating. It was more relaxing than Cutter would have imagined it could be. Even Sandy smiled a lot.

A couple of days later, Hugh showed up at Cutter's house. He presented Cutter with a check. Sort of a going away gift, he told Cutter. As a thank you for his services. The commission members had all kicked in, especially Geren Randolph who had taken great pleasure from the besting of Ty Carroll. Cutter looked at the amount and smiled and thanked Hugh profusely. He had had to turn in his city car of course, and this check was large enough he could buy a used car. In fact, the next morning he went down to the local dealer and picked out an older, but low mileage, used Wrangler. He'd never gotten over giving up his first one and this just felt like home, somehow.

The first week of January, Cutter packed a suitcase and threw it into the Jeep. He went back inside and finished putting a last few items in a backpack. He stood in the foyer and Sandy and the kids joined him. He squatted down and asked Jordan, "What's the first rule?"

"Don't get hurt," she answered.

He turned to Livingston and asked, "What's rule number two?"

"Don't get hurt," Livingston answered proudly.

"Close enough." Turned back to Jordan and said, "Number three?"

"Take care of your brother."

"And your mother. Remember that part," he told her. Then to Livingston, "And what's the most important rule?"

Livingston laughed, "I know, I know. Have fun."

"That's right. You guys be good and I'll see you soon. Remember how much I love you." He stood and faced Sandy.

"What should I do?" she asked.

Cutter bit his lip to avoid uttering the Rhett Butler line. When that feeling had passed, he told her, "I'll write when I get work."

He hugged each of the kids tightly, threw the dog a dirty look and walked to the Jeep. He tossed the backpack onto the passenger seat and climbed in, closed the door and started the engine. He put his hands on top of the steering wheel and his forehead on his hands. He sat that way for what seemed like a long time. Being in this car, backpack beside him, took him back to another day of change, back on Hatteras Island. He smiled and moved the Jeep on down the road.

ACKNOWLEDGEMENTS

It turned out writing a second book was easier for me than writing the first one. In part, easier because I felt more comfortable with the process. But more importantly because I recognized the huge contributions others have to make for an idea to turn into a story, a story into a manuscript and a manuscript into a book. Again, a huge thanks to my muse, critic, editor and wife, Deborah, who seems to be able to solve any problem, from plot to punctuation, in a manner that is supportive and helpful. She makes me glad to be me. Also again, thank you to all the wonderful folks at Appalachian Acorn Publishing, especially Samantha Varner. Their willingness to read the manuscript, make suggestions, offer feedback and get the book out make it a pleasure being in the business. A big thank you to those who made a special contribution to this book: Patti Hicks. She read each chapter as it was finished and offered valuable feedback and commentary. She asked the questions which made sure all plot and character details were properly attended to. Jake Barney. He provided the photo used to create the cover of the book. The photograph was taken in Jake's adopted state of Colorado where he spends every minute not at work either skiing or mountain climbing. Will Dersken. The model in Jake's photo. Will gave up his last run of the day to pose for the cover. Tad Barney. He took Jake's photo, worked his magic, and turned it into the graphic for the cover, which he also designed. Tad makes us all look good. Finally, to my family. Like Cutter, I was blessed to be part of a large, loving and supportive family.

One problem I did encounter was creating names for a large cast of characters. I've always admired those writers who can do this. Dickens was a genius at it, though no character names ever topped Yossarian or Bilbo Baggins. To avoid the hassle, I appropriated a number of names of friends and relatives. So a special thanks goes out to Alicia Lein, Jerry and Suzie Picker, Charlie Dwan, Chris Bugg, Kaitlyn Reinan, Patti and Tom Hicks, Laurie Loftus, Kathy Jones, Jacob Matthew (Barney), Sabrina (Khouri), Theano (Stavrinos), Sarah (Randall-Cline), Steve Barker, Wade Taylor, Rob Fellure, Bradford Q(uicksall), (Ken) A. Jones, Constitutional Lawyer, Lois Borin, Paul Timothy (Barney), Beth Chamberlin, Christopher Carroll (Barney), Whitney Husz, Ken Dunn, John and Becky (Barney), Cathy Rose (Barney), Phil (Buckle), Carson (Huston), Jordan and Justin Callaham, Molly (Wilkinson) and Brian Cheffer.

Made in the USA
Columbia, SC
07 October 2018